BRIAN'S BIRTHDAY BLOODBATH

Brian G. Berry

ISBN-13: 9798351358086
ISBN-10: 1477123456

Cover design by: Drew Stepek
Library of Congress Control Number: 2018675309
Printed in the United States of America

Dedicated to Tim Curran and his character Grimshanks, the most EVIL clown ever conceived.

CONTENTS

PROLOGUE

For ten years he'd been locked up behind those walls, behind that steel plated door with the oblique slot that allowed the guards to peek in at him, to keep an eye on him; make sure he wasn't up to something funny. The cell that confined him smelled of things—things like sour piss and boiled feces, old blood, and unwashed bodies. Daily, the men in white suits would come in there and prepare him for the doctor. One of them, a guard, would put a shotgun on him with a grin, while the other, a nurse, chained him to the wall and put something in his vein that made his legs and arms go weak. The doctor would come in after the solution worked its alchemy in him, then draw up a chair, seat himself and start speaking to the man, asking him things. One of the most favored questions he would ask the man was why he favored children over adults. The man chained to the wall would crack a grin like a moldering corpse, and recount his reasons by impressing upon the doctor vivid and terrible images. All this the doctor would absorb with an abject twist in his reactions. But, the man, beneath the spell of the injected fluid, would only grin, smile in the way he used to smile when his face was painted up like a clown, back when he used to entertain at children's parties—uninvited.

But that was a long time ago, back when he was free and liberated, able to do those things he liked doing to both kids and adults.

They called him a monster in the papers; a demon. It was shared between children in whispers at sleepovers that he was the scratching sound on the closet door, the cackle and slanted red eyes beneath the bed. It was rumored that if you conjured his name in the mirror three times when the wind blew right and the moon hung in a star-flecked sky, he would appear, not as an apparition appears to haunt your mind, but as a tapping on the window, or a scuttle across the roof. But he wasn't always such a bad man. Many moons ago, before people started calling him Bones the Clown, on account that's all he left behind of those who died screaming beneath his filed teeth, he was known as Kyle Cohen.

—

Back when Kyle was but a child of thirteen summers, he was in the backseat of his parent's cherry red Buick, paging through a comic book. It was pretty late, so it was plenty dark outside, but as always, he had his flashlight with him so he didn't have to read in the faint moonlight pouring through the back window.

They were on their way home from a movie, driving along a single-lane stretch that was bracketed by thick stands of cottonwoods and birch, a few blackened homes set back from the road. There was a car awkwardly parked on the side of the road up ahead, the emergency lights winking redly in the dark. It was at a slight angle to suggest that maybe the driver had avoided crashing into a loping deer or some rogue object on the road, judging by the fresh black streaks on the pavement trailing behind its tires.

Kyle's dad, Peter, slowed his speed. He had a habit of helping folks down on their luck, so he pulled the Buick over behind the parked car, set the brake, grabbed Kyle's flashlight, and exited the car. His mom, Mary, told Peter that it was probably a bad idea, and it didn't look like anyone was around anyhow, so maybe they should just leave. But, Peter just wanted to make certain nothing bad had happened to the occupants—he was a good man like that.

Both Kyle and his mom watched after him, watching him search through the windows of the car, then spray the trees with the flashlight in a quick flick of his wrist like maybe he saw something moving around out there in those thickets.

He rounded the hood of the car, and started heading down over to a patch of woods and, upon seeing this, Mary rolled down the window and shouted at him not to go in there. But Peter told her he would only be a second and there was no reason for her to sound worried like she was beginning to. Mary didn't like it and said she had a bad feeling about all of this, and Kyle, too, was feeling a bit apprehensive himself. For what reason? It was never established. Perhaps the black encroaching reach of the night added to it. Maybe the way the wind blew, coupled with the necrotic face of the moon. The movie they had seen, a creature feature involving ghoulish, subterranean grave eaters, helped to aggregate the night with its substance; all the ingredients that imbibe the horror film were now material and animate outside the Buick.

Kyle was watching after the flashlight blade bobbing and sweeping the woods when all of sudden it went out like a blown candle. Mary stifled a yelp in her throat. She rolled down the window again and shouted to her husband out into the black, windy night. She waited only briefly for a reply, and after none found her—none but the sound of heavy birch and cottonwood boughs swishing with the wind— she began in a stuttering vocal to tell Kyle not to worry; that everything was okay, and that his father must have accidentally dropped the light and its bulb shattered and he would be heading back to the car right about now with a smile on his face. It all sounded like she was trying to convince herself more than anything else.

The wait brought a dreadful perception to the mind.

Minute's ground by, and Mary broke the tense silence with a string of words that were both confusing and frightening. All at once, she was fidgeting in her seat, her finger stabbing at the window, gasps of shrill cries in her words. Seized by a sudden tremor, Kyle searched outside the window, but all was black and shadowed. Kyle told his mother that he couldn't see anything and that she was beginning to scare him. But Mary either ignored her son or was so distraught by the image that filled her pupils a moment before, that she scooted over and settled behind the wheel. She shouted out in frustration after her fingers grabbed air where the keys should have been in the ignition. She hastily searched the floor and beneath the seat. Even inspecting the visor.

During a lull in her aggravation, Kyle prompted her with questions; asked what it was she had seen outside in the night; he was wondering why she suddenly became frightened—she was reacting as though she was witness to some lurking, forest horror of inhuman contours and dripping fangs. He told her he was afraid because she was afraid, and her shaking added shivers to his skin.

She calmed enough to speak, but before she did, she glanced out all the windows, a frightful mask on her face. And with a face as pale as cream; in a voice choked with a dreadful frequency, she said: "*Clown* … I saw a clown. It was covered in blood."

A clown? Wet in blood? Kyle's complexion frosted white, a cold chilled his blood and iced his bones. Shivers ran along his body and black dots jumped in his eyes.

Then something hit the car.

Mary stopped crying. Kyle sat immobile as the

moon.

Silence held their ears, all but for the sounds of his mother whimpering and wind blowing through the trees and washing up against the car.

Something hit the car again, and this time, Mary jumped with a scream.

"The lights," she whispered in unbelief. "One of the headlights is gone."

Kyle swallowed a scream, but it was immature, because then he screamed after a sound—louder and stronger than before—rocked the car on its springs, and the remaining headlight blew out black. Darkness settled, and only because of the red points of the flashers from the car ahead, did it not swallow over the two of them like waves beneath the sea. As it was, it brought a more sinister note to the night, as strobing effects of the red lights knifed the interior of the Buick like a mist of blood.

Mary sobbed and choked out words that Kyle could not understand. She watched with widened, terror-stricken eyes at the clown flashing in red, and she knew it wanted her to *see* it. Its shamble was timed with the lights.

Kyle had balled himself down to the floor, his knees together at his chin. His mother was whimpering and shaking and Kyle had no strength to hear it anymore. He plugged his ears to the best of his ability, but her voice carried to him, and it sounded much like voices do when you're underwater, so Kyle pressed his palms tighter to his skull.

Then she screamed; a terrible scream with a pitch that had enough volume behind it to crack glass.

Kyle sprang up like he had a knife driven up inside of him, and started shaking his mother's shoulders, demanding she stops screaming as she was. But, then he saw what had encouraged her mounting terror. Outside, standing before the hood, spoked redly in the flashing lights, was a naked man, a face painted white, eyes greased in bold black circles, and a frown of smeared crimson. Poking out alongside his temples were tufts of greenish, cotton hair. His body was a sheen of red coating—a bloody oil, and it dotted parts of his white painted face. There was something in his fist, and Kyle recognized the implement: a hammer, and caught in its claw was a ball of stringy hair. His *fathers*.

It was too much to look on any amount of time without screaming. And Mary screamed, unleashing the horror of the image before her in a strident, piercing wail.

As madness engulfed her mind, she swung open the door, left the car, and raced into the road. Kyle screamed at his abandonment in the backseat, his hands and face pressed to the window.

She made it about halfway across the road when the naked, blood-greased clown chased after her and swung on her head with the hammer. Instantly her legs stiffened and she went down on her face, limp as a boiled noodle.

Kyle pounded on the window, screaming as only a child could scream. But his voice weakened a pitch as the clown lowered himself over his mother, and a cold wave streaked up Kyle's back as the clown tugged at his mother's pants until the fabric was a roll at her ankles.

The clown rose out of his crouch and faced Kyle, his fingers curled around his penis and worked up the shaft until it was a solid point. Kyle blanched and turned away, curled down in the backseat, unable to shake the obscene image from his eyes. It was only after a moment did he recuperate enough strength and rise to glance outside the window. The clown was on top of his mother, his body gyrating and grinding with fierce strokes. The hammer in his fist fell on his mother in a sickening repetition. Kyle averted his eyes, and with the immediacy of madness in his veins, he struck out for the door across from him, reached for the lever, and pulled.

The door swung open wide, assisted by the slight slant of the Buick. Outside, he faced the shadow-crawling woods, and their long, sinuous trunks branched above him in a crown of gnarled limbs.

A wind blew against him and brought with it the sound of footsteps. Kyle turned, but it was a slow and gradual turn, like facing the emerging, breathing horror from a closet.

Kyle pissed himself when the clown filled his eyes. Standing as he was, beside the Buick, his penis hard and bloody, the shafting red flashes traced around his narrow figure. He held out a fist, and in it, was a ball of ropy strings like skinned serpents. Kyle attempted to run, to turn and race into the woods, but so compounded by fear and the horror of the man, that he found his legs anchored to the ground.

He started to plea to the clown as the blood-slicked figure started walking toward him. The clown stopped and regarded the young boy with a glare absent of pity. It was a mask of evil. A pernicious glare. He held out the slimy ball of ropes and Kyle reeled, his stomach churning, his body shaking. Close as he was, Kyle could smell the man, and it was the redolence of decay, of death and rot and exhumed graves of pestilential bodies. The grim combination blew off him like a pall of poison with the wind. But it was when the clown brought up the ball of gore to his red mouth, and his teeth, pointed like the teeth of some monstrous ogre, sank into the clump, and blood juiced from his chin, that Kyle fell to his knees, a vacant and illusory expression on his face. The sound of the meat clamped between those filed points was an obscene and repulsive sound. His stomach roiled as he watched, enraptured by such a hideous sight.

Finished with his meal, the clown sucked down the blood and bits of tissue off his fingers, then pointed one long bony finger down at the boy. His lips peeled back on those blood-stained fangs, and a laugh like a demon's dissonance blew from his throat. Kyle tried to scream, but his stomach pumped up all the candy and popcorn he had eaten back at the movies, and it came out in a gelid fountain to splash at his knees.

The clown continued to point those red fingers at

the boy and laugh.

Kyle rolled to this side and with his arms extended, he fingered the soil and began to crawl towards the woods.

His ankle was instantly seized, and he felt himself being dragged up the soft acclivity of the earth and onto the roughened tarmac of the road.

Dumped beside his mother, Kyle saw the mutilation. Her body, a ruin of slaughter, lay framed in a wide pool of blood. Her head was spread out in a gristly ring of meat and bone that looked as though a mallet had crushed her skull. Carved along her back were deep channels gored by the claw of the hammer. Above her hips were holes, crudely hacked as though a beast had taken great bites of her flesh. Entrails streamed from the gashes like the bodies of bloated red worms. Blood painted the white of her legs red, and her anus looked to have been enlarged by the hammer too.

Shaken by the state of his mother, he failed to see the clown walk past him.

In his bloody hand, the clown took his cock and greased the length of it a darker red. He straddled the woman and pissed on her back. It was a heavy stream and its touch splashed against Mary, causing steam to rise out of her many wounds. Directing his stream to her anus, he filled her body and the sound was like water bubbling in a drain. He leaned back and laughed up to the stars.

Kyle felt his bladder loosen and his bowels release in his pants.

It was all too much. To face such absolute, mind-rending horror as what filled his eyes, his mind, it opened up things inside of you. Things that should never be, back from a time when the horrors receded beneath the sea. Now, his mind had seen what none should. And in place was a black void peopled with haunting shapes. All innocence had melted beneath a terrible reality. Kyle was no longer in control. He watched as a thrall watches his master. The clown rubbed his cock in blood and black gore. He reached inside Mary's body and came out with a fistful of dripping meat.

He fed Kyle.

And Kyle sat there, distant from what he watched and ate. The noxious fumes had no effect, and his body ate as he was fed. Gas bulged his stomach, and when a heap of bones lay on the black road gutted of sinew and flesh, he felt the hands tug at his pants, and something hard jammed into him—then a blow to his head sent his mind into a vortex of night.

—

After that night, Kyle was taken somewhere; to where, he hadn't the faintest clue. But it was dark and musty, not a hint of daylight speared the room. The walls were made out of cinder blocks and taped to them were photographs of children and posters of clowns, some with children, others posing with blades and hatchets, blood on their faces; yet others had flowers and balloons. It was a veritable clogging of prints that made your head spin with speculation. There was a soiled mattress in the corner of the room in which he spent his nights, chained to the wall.

The clown came down there every now and again and taught him things, did things to him that further imperiled his sanity. But after a few years passed, Kyle was no longer human—no trace of humanistic quality resided in his bones. He had been converted, forged into something that resembled neither man nor beast. His mind had glimpsed fantastic and dreaded realms. Pain had disfigured his emotions and neither needle, blade, or violation was felt.

During a particularly heavy night of drinking, the clown descended the steps into the cellar, which was Kyle's den.

Kyle was sitting on his bed, his back flat against the clown sheeted wall. The clown said something to him, and Kyle figured he knew what it meant. He had to position himself like he did so many nights. And to make matters easy for the clown, Kyle was never allowed to dress himself. And if he needed to piss or shit, that's what the bucket beside his mattress was for.

Staggering further into the cellar, the clown pulled from his bottle, his other hand working his shaft. He said something again that Kyle hadn't heard, because Kyle was doing something that required him to focus, preparing himself. As the clown lowered closer, Kyle swung out with a piece of metal he had shaved down to a fine point. It struck the clown in the eye, but Kyle, so embalmed with red rage, struck him again in the throat, jabbing a line of dots in his neck that pissed out thin wires of blood.

The clown was clutching at his neck as blood pressed thickly between his fingers. He went face down on the mattress, gutturally choking on blood. Kyle continued stabbing at the man, poking him in the back of the neck, in the head, wherever the shaved point was able to pierce. It took a moment, but eventually the man stopped moving.

Kyle managed to free himself from the chains binding him to the wall after he poked around in the lock with the metal file.

He left the man behind, not bothering to look back or to make sure he was really dead. It didn't matter. What mattered to Kyle was leaving this place. But before he did that, he had to prepare himself for the world he had left behind so many years before.

His search of the house turned up some of the objects he would carry with him into the future. There was the clown suit, a silky white jumper with black polka dots running over it. A pair of black clown shoes. There was a container of make-up and he used it to paint his face white, and ring his eyes a thick black. He smeared crimson around his lips. Over the years, he was kept bald, and so he painted his pate white.

Armed with a hammer, the very hammer used to butcher his mother and father, he also grabbed himself a big blade from the cutlery block in the kitchen. And with that, he left behind that charnel mad house of violation and screams.

He later slipped into a thicket of oaks, eventually coming across two boys about his age. What he had become manifested itself in a rampage that caught the two young men off guard. There wasn't much left of them by the time they were discovered. Forensics' first assumption was that some coyotes had gotten to them after they were dead, but upon further examination, they found the teeth marks were human. The two were little more than sinew and bone.

It was to be the first two cannibal kills in a grisly chain that would tally into innumerable dead by Bones the Clown.

CHAPTER 1

1990

The doctor was coming again, he could smell him. Bones the Clown cocked his head like he always did when the smell of the man filled the corridor outside his room. He could hear the chains lapping the knee of his preceding visitors.

The oblique hatch was thrown open, and a pair of eyes filled the port.

"Back against the wall asshole," a voice said. "Make it snappy."

The bolt on the door was unlatched and it swung open. The guard with the shotgun was first, followed by his partner with the needle.

"You move in a manner I feel is liable to threaten myself or my partner here, and I'll empty this thing in you," shotgun-man said.

Bones grinned; that same grin he always gave them guards and staff—especially the doctor.

After they bound him, the needle was pressed into his vein. He felt the juice mix with his blood. He'd been having that shot so long, that it was getting to the point he was developing a tolerance.

But he wasn't one to inform the staff of such things. They waited a moment until they felt he was spongy enough to see the doctor. Shotgun-man was chewing on something, the barrel leveled with the Cohen, his finger crooked on the trigger.

Bones rolled his eyes as though he were polluted inside, drifting into ethereal landscapes as the elixir coursed along his veins.

"He's ready," the nurse said.

Shotgun-man backed up into the corridor. "He's ready, Doc."

The sound of heels stamping the corridor echoed around off the walls of the cell. Bones' head was wheeling as though he were rocking gently on a boat.

Doctor Green filled the door frame. "All, Mr. Cohen, I see your medicine has kicked in. This is good." He dragged in a chair and seated himself in it. "How are you feeling today, Kyle?"

Bones narrowed a glare on the doctor that was cold as the blood in his body. He never spoke much, instead, he made sounds that a sane man would find disturbing. Sometimes he laughed—a cruel, wicked cackle like you would imagine a demon clown to sound like. There was no mirth or humor in it. Just a frightful sort of peal that rose and fell as though myriad voices competed in frightening vibrations.

"I imagine you are feeling much like you were yesterday, hmm?" Doctor Green smiled at the man. "I realize you have been at my facility for longer than any patient of mine, and during that time I have not had the pleasure of hearing you speak. Will you ever speak to me, Kyle?"

Bones softened his glare as though he was contemplating allowing this doctor entry to his mind, but, a gradual shift in his expression altered his face, and it was a twisted glare with trembling lips. His eyes rolled back white, and a bar of foam pushed past his lips. His body shook with tremors.

Green was on his feet, demanding the assistance of his nurse. Shotgun-man looked on with a curling grin.

Bones was thrashing violently, and the nurse was having difficulty controlling the man's increasing spasms. "I don't know what's wrong doctor, he doesn't seem to be—" Bones went still. The nurse stepped back. "Doctor ..."

Green stepped up. He reached out a finger to test for a pulse.

"There's a pulse—wait—"

Green screamed at the sudden pressure crushing his hand. Bones' teeth clamped like a steel plate of spikes on the doctor's fingers. Hysterical, he began to squeal, and sweat stood out on his brow; he wrenched his arm, but the pain was too much and he stood there in agony as blood filled Bones' mouth and streaked down his chin in stringing beads.

Shotgun-man came forward. "Move aside, doc, I got this sonofabitch!" He shouldered the gun, drew a line, and jerked the trigger.

Anticipating the move, Bones shifted quickly, dragging Green over to shield him. The explosion was deafening, and its blast fatal, as Green was torn open from clavicle to breastbone. Blood splashed the wall, and oiled Bones red. A wicked, crimson-greased grin peeled open, and his eyes fell on the guard.

Shocked by the death of Green, the guard failed to chamber another shell in time as Bones sprang up, tethered by the chain, but able to reach out, he grabbed the shotgun, ran the slide, and hit the guard with a blast that splashed his face into the ceiling.

The nurse was screaming, crawling on the floor, at a loss of his feet as blood and meat slicked the ground. Bones pumped another shell, but instead of firing on the man, he beat him down; hammered at his head until it broke open like a rotten melon. Brains sludged out and at the sight, Bones the Clown became enticed and hungry. He crouched, reached out, and ran his fingers in it, enjoying the feel of it. He scooped up a warm clump with his fingers and crammed it in his mouth. The juices flooded his jaw and streamed down his throat. Rejuvenated by the taste, he turned and faced the wall. The shotgun thundered and his chains were free. Racking the pump, Bones the Clown stepped into the corridor.

Alarms rang and neighboring patients battered at their doors and shouted. He raced down the corridor, down the way he was lead every morning to the yard.

He corned at the end and ran into a guard who was shocked at the sight of the man covered in blood. Bones grinned and the weapon cracked, shearing the man from crotch to armpit; his body slid apart in two bloody slabs.

Chambering a shell, he ran, and his strides never weakened, even as he dashed headlong into another armed man. Bones was quick, and without stopping, the weapon rocked and the man was a stain on the wall.

The door to the exterior grounds was ahead. He leveled the weapon and shattered the lock. The weapon empty, he kept it as an object to wield.

Outside, the sun was bright and its power burned his eyes. Blinking, staggering, he ran as though the very imps of hell were on his heels. He was headed for the fence which was a wall of wire crowned with barbs. A man screamed at him, and he turned and leveled the gun on him. It was another guard, and this man froze, dropping his pistol to the grass.

"Please, no!" he pleaded.

Bones the Clown shuffled over to him, inverted the gun, and swung its stock into the man's skull. His head fragmented and blood flared at impact. Dropping the shotgun, he reached out for the pistol and jammed it in his pants. He leaped onto the fence and clambered up its diamond notches until his arms reached higher and were tangled by the barbs. But so toughened by his violation over the years, the pain a lesser man would feel, did not hinder his escape.

Through the nest of barbed wire, he crawled, and once he leaped from the top down to the other side of the fence, his body was a lacerated coat of sores, bleeding and streaking.

He was a red flash as his legs wheeled, and he sought the refuge of a field spotted in patches of brush and cottonwoods.

After ten years of imprisonment, Bones the Clown was now free. Liberated to wander and eat, and he was plenty starving.

CHAPTER 2

Brian may have had higher hopes for his presents from his parents, but he was satisfied with what he received. He did end up getting a new game for his Nintendo, so that was a good thing. It was Commando, a *Capcom* game. After he opened it and saw the image of a soldier in green fatigues, a rifle in his hand, explosions behind him, and the granite-faced font of Commando, he smiled and tore up the steps, placed it in his console, thumbed the power button and hadn't removed himself since. That is until his dad came to his door the moment he was tossing grenades at machine gun bunkers and avoiding pixelated bullets.

"Brian," his dad said, pushing the door open. "You're mother and I are headed out for the evening. But I want you to—"

"Does that mean Travis and Billy can't come over?" Brian interrupted, pausing his game.

"Of course not," his dad told him. "As I was saying, *birthday boy*, your mother and I are going out for a while, but we have Jessica coming over to watch you three tonight."

"Jessica?" Brian beamed. That would surely make the night better. He had a crush on Jessica since she started watching him five years ago, back when he was seven years old. She was thirteen at the time. She was graduating high school this year last he heard, and she had a boyfriend, Jack—a big jock type who always had some lame-ass comment to say about his football team. But Brian didn't care. He was working an angle; he would get Jessica at some point; he felt it in his bones. She was lovely. Not too tall and not too short, she had a pair of titties on her that made it hard not to stare. And she always wore these tight-fitting shirts that didn't leave much to the imagination. Her hair was red and long and she wore it down her shoulders in thick curls. Her eyes were green and big and they always sparkled when they landed on Brian.

"That's right, son. She should be here soon, but if she's not—" he pointed a finger at his son, his glare serious "—*you're* in charge."

Brian smiled.

"But that doesn't mean you do whatever you want, you hear?"

Brian nodded. "Can I order pizza at least?"

"Jessica said she was bringing a pizza with her, so she has dinner covered. You're free to polish off the cake, but make sure you share with your friends—speaking of, when are they supposed to arrive?"

"Uh, I think any minute now," Brian said, checking the face of his new Casio watch.

Brian's dad checked his watch too. "It's almost

five, so I'm guessing five?"

"Yeah, Travis said he would be here after his mom got off work, and she gets off at 4:30 or something, and Billy said he would be here around the same time. So …"

"Okay, that works. I left the number to the restaurant your mother and I are headed to on the fridge. We'll be staying out quite late; we're seeing a show after we eat. So don't expect us home until around two in the morning. I told Jessica to expect a late night. We'll call before we head back. Any questions?"

Brian shook his head. "Nope."

"Okay. Well, happy birthday son. Did you enjoy your gifts?"

Brian unpaused his game. "Yes, very much. I love this game, just wish—well, nothing."

"What is it?"

"I was just hoping for Mega Man, too, but it's okay. I know it costs a lot of money for these games."

Brian's dad smiled and leaned in for a whisper. "I'll tell you a secret, son … Your grandmother is sending you that game in the mail—but you didn't hear that from me!"

Brian paused the game again. "Really?"

"That's right—should be here next week."

"Awesome! Thanks, dad!"

"Whoa, don't thank me—better write your grandma a letter, let her know how grateful you are.

"I will, I will!"

Brian went back to his game, a big smile on his

face.

"Well, I'm headed out—oh, hi honey."

Brian's mom walked into the room, and the smell of her perfume, a rose-scented potion, followed her. "Brian, are you going to be okay here with Jessica?"

Brian laughed. "Of course, mom—she's awesome!"

She laughed in return. "You still have a crush on her, huh?"

Brian's face flushed red. "*No*, I don't have a crush on her!"

"Don't embarrass him, dear," his father said, smiling.

"I'm not *embarrassed*."

"We'll leave you to it," his dad said.

His mom crouched and put her arms around Brian's shoulders, squeezing him tight. "You have a good night, sweetheart, and did your father tell you that we left—"

"Yes, yes—the number is downstairs on the fridge, you're getting me killed here, mom!"

"Killed? It's a video game," she said, confused.

Brian rolled his eyes. "You wouldn't get it."

She kissed him lightly on the head and stepped out of the room. His father patted his head. "Happy birthday, son."

"Yeah, you too dad," Brian said, engrossed in his game.

His dad smiled and walked out of the room. Their footsteps receded down the stairs, and they were still saying goodbye but he ignored them. A moment later, the door shut hard like it always did.

Brian was facing a horde of soldiers who were determined to end one of his lives. He tossed a grenade of pixels but it failed to kill the soldiers. Their white bullets crossed the screen and his character flashed away.

"Damnit!"

CHAPTER 3

The doorbell chimed, not once or twice, but a rapid-fire beat that rang through the house, annoying Brian to no end. He paused his game and ran out of his room and raced down the stairs. He grabbed at the door and swung it open.

"About time, turd face," Travis said.

"Shut up."

"Did you get it?"

"*Mega Man?*"

Travis nodded.

"Yeah, my grandma got it for me, but it won't be here until next week. I did get commando though!"

"Next week? That really sucks. But commando I heard is awesome!"

"It's pretty fun—come inside already."

Travis shuffled into the foyer, his red bag shouldered. "Is Billy here yet?"

"Not yet—he should be here soon though."

"Cool—you won't believe what I brought along."

Intrigued, Brian asked: "What is it?"

"I'll show you when Billy gets here."

Right then the doorbell chimed.

"Well, looks like he's here," Brian said. He swung the door back. "Billy!"

"Happy birthday, Brian! Sorry I couldn't make it earlier—here."

Brian took the present offered to him. It was in yellow matte wrapping with a purple bow. "Great wrapping job," he told Billy.

"My mom did it."

Brian scratched it open. "Oh, awesome! How did you—"

"My dad bought me a copy after my mom already bought me one, so I gave you the extra before they took it back to the store."

"*Castlevania!*" Brian said, searching its cover. "I've heard great things about this one."

"Yeah, it's really fun but hard."

"Like all these games," Brian stated.

"Want to see my present, Brian?" Travis asked.

"Duh—let me see it."

Travis reached into his bag. "Upstairs."

The three of them ran up the steps, Brian whining about what was so important about it that he has to show him in the bedroom.

Once they got into Brian's room, Billy sat down on the bed, his bag beside him, and Travis stood in the middle of the room and pulled out his present with a big, dopey smile on his face. It was a thick stack of nudey magazines. The covers were illustrated with big-breasted women and hairy patches between their legs. Some were swallowing things.

Brian looked at the magazines with a pair of

widened eyes. "Where did you *get* these?"

Travis laughed. "I stole them from my brother."

"*Dale?* He'll kill you if he finds out."

"He ain't going to find out. But pretty neat though, right?"

"I have never seen one, well, I never held one—I've seen plenty on the magazine racks at the store, but this is crazy. I can't keep these—my mom would flip out if she found these."

Travis looked hurt. "Then *hide* them somewhere, you idiot."

"Like where?"

"Your fathers shed out back?"

Brian nodded. "Good thinking—the place he's *always* at, you *idiot*."

"How about underneath the shed?" Billy suggested. "Like put 'em in a bag or something—that way they won't get all moldy and wet."

"Now *that's* an idea," Travis said.

Billy took one and paged through it. "Well, this beats my gift," he said sourly.

"Hardly," Brian said. "I've always wanted to play Castlevania!"

"You would rather play that game than play with these!" Travis said as he thrust out a centerfold of a busty blond posing on the hood of a Ferrari.

"I can't play with a magazine," Brian told Travis. "Besides, Jessica is coming over, and *that's* my woman."

"Jessica? You mean Jack's Jessica?" Billy asked.

Brian turned and landed a fist on Billy's shoulder.

"*My* Jessica, and don't you forget it."

"You're eleven—"

Brian hit him again. "Twelve, you dumbass."

"When is she supposed to be here?" Travis asked, a smile on his face.

"Soon."

"Oh man, Jessica and a pile of magazines—she has great tits," Travis remarked.

Brian leaped on him and took him to the ground. Travis was laughing as Brian roughed him up. "Okay, man, she's yours—but she does have a nice rack."

Travis ducked out of the way as Brian came at him again. It was all fun of course. They were all best friends and had been since they were in kindergarten together. All the same age, Travis was the biggest of the three. He had short brown hair that was never really brushed, like something a hand just ruffles after waking up. His face was a bit pudgy as was his body. He liked to think he was the enforcer of their small group—that if anyone stood between his friends, he would bash 'em down into a pulp.

Billy was a more bookish type. He was thin and had blond hair that was always neatly combed and he always wore shorts no matter the time of the year. He wore glasses and the lenses always showed off his eyes as big brown spots.

Brian wasn't as thin as Billy, and not as pudgy as Travis. He was in-between when it came to their weights. He had short brown hair that he generally wore back in thick spikes; he had blue eyes and loved to play video games.

All three were considered nerds, but it was a mark of honor to them. They enjoyed their comic books and video games and trashy movies. It was what they did and loved, and if that made them different from everyone else, then fuck it. It was the better option.

"What do you guys want to do?" Brian asked them.

"How about we play some Castlevania? I'll show you some stuff I found," Billy said, leaving the bed and scooting on the ground closer to the television.

"That sounds good to me," Travis agreed. "You two *morons* play the games, I'll look through these magazines for a while."

"Okay," Brian said. "I'd rather play the game any way you perv. But make sure you hide that shit when Jessica gets here. I don't want her to think I'm some weirdo like you."

Travis jumped onto Brian's bed, kicked his shoes off, and started thumbing through the pages of a magazine titled: *Big Un's*.

Brian slotted the game after removing the Commando cartridge and placing it back into its black sheath.

Billy was already explaining to Brian what to avoid in the game and what special weapons and potions to use.

The night was pressing on the house, but it was still light enough that a faint purple sky showed outside the window. It was getting windy outside, and starting to blow and ruffle at the trees and brush against the house.

Though Brian was excited to jump into Castlevania and see what it was about, he couldn't wait for Jessica to arrive.

CHAPTER 4

"Hurry up, Gary, I don't have all fucking night—I gotta' be at Kristy's by seven."

"Shut your goddamn yapper, I'm almost finished here." Gary shook out the last drops of piss into a thatch of weeds at the base of an oak. Fixing himself, he backed up and turned around, only to jump at the sight of a man standing there. "Jesus Christ, Carl, you almost gave me a fucking heart attack—what the hell you doing anyways, sneaking up on me like that in the dark, you know I got a bad heart."

The figure stood there, blackened by the shade of the oak, drowned by the night.

"Wait a minute," Gary said unsure of himself, feeling something funny in the air. "Who the hell—"

The muted figure raised an arm and a flash drew the night away. Before Gary's face fragmented like a broken wine jug, he saw somebody covered in blood, a grin of spiked teeth.

"Gary! Christ, what the hell was that?" Carl shouted, dropping his cigarette to the gravel. "Gary?" Unable to see much of anything beyond his truck, he reached into his cab and came back out with a flashlight. He popped it and the blade sliced a shaft in the night, the weeds shifted in leaning shadow. "Gary!"

Feeling strange, he reached back into his rig, curled his fingers around the hilt of a hunting knife out, held it at his side. There were coyotes and things of that nature out here, it was good to be prepared. But whatever made that sound surely wasn't an animal. It sounded like a gunshot, only muffled.

"This better not be a fucking joke, man."

Something filled his beam in the shape of a man, then slipped behind a tree.

Carl jumped back a step. "Gary, that you? Come on out of there! Stop playing around—I saw you run behind that tree, asshole."

Carl narrowed his eyes over the flashlight drawing its beam slowly through the weeds and gradually sweeping between the oaks. A branch snapped to his right, and the light fell on the spot he thought it came from.

In a soft voice, he said: "Gary?" He took a couple of steps forward, his knees parting the weeds. "Enough of this game, what the hell was that noise, Gary? I swear to God if you're fucking with me, I'm gonna crack your balls!"

Panning his light to the left, the beam fell on a man a foot away from him. "Fuck me!"

The pistol flashed and smoked. Carl's face impacted, muffling the explosion. His body crumpled like an empty pillow sack.

Bones sheathed the pistol in his waistband, bent over, and grabbed the knife. He ran his finger along its edge. It was sharp, but he needed to test it on something meatier. Folding back a flap of Carl's flannel, he sank its point into the hairy belly button. The blades incision was a juicy note as it sank to the hilt, and with a powerful jerk of his arm, he sheared the man open to the throat. Blood pumped from the channel in a red wave. Bones widened the gap with his hand, pulling back a mat of hairy flesh. His fingers crawled inside, grabbing hold of something solid and wet. There was a resistance to whatever it was, and Bones worked the blade around his fingers slicing through thick rubbery tubes and scratching bone. It was loose now, and Bones brought it out of the cavity in a dripping clod. It was the heart, and the sight of it put meat on Bones' cock. He brought it to his mouth and his fangs pierced the muscle, tearing a hole in it like an apple.

Crouched over the man like he was, he made quite the image. It was something out of a Goya painting; a ghoulish, pale thing hunched over something dead, its face painted red with blood. The moon was out overhead and it gave the scene a frightening ignition.

After he finished eating, he walked up to the truck, went around, and jumped inside—right behind the wheel. It was an old, faded, blue Chevy model. The keys were in the ignition and he turned them over. The engine roared to life. Grabbing the knob on the gearshift, he put it in drive and slowly pulled onto the dark road.

Bones kept his pace with the speed limit, but after around thirty minutes, something up ahead caused him to slow. It was a couple of police cars blocking the road, their blue and red flashes lighting up the night. There was a trail of road flares strung along the blacktop directing drivers onto the shoulder, and two indistinct black shapes he knew to be cops were out there waving flashlights, indicating he should pull aside.

But Bones increased his speed.

The beams of the flashlights were swinging and wheeling back and forth in agitation now.

Bones pressed on the accelerator with his bare foot; the Chevy was a bulky black missile, growling as it hurtled toward the two officers.

He couldn't hear it, but Bones knew they were taking shots at him from the flames jetting from pistol barrels. A bullet chipped the windshield to his right, then another landed a few inches to the left. He kept his head low as more bullets drilled the windshield in a staggering line.

Then Bones was suddenly shaken behind the wheel as the fender crunched against something— a couple of things—and he felt something catch and drag at the wheels. He slowed down and came to a stop after fifty feet.

Stepping out into the cool night, the moon above him, he looked back up to the roadblock, to the police cars. A long red smear trailed behind the Chevy like a barrel of red paint exploded in a wide, splattered column.

He inspected beneath the truck and saw something like strips of meat and gristle and bone caught up in the axles, some hair stringing from the chassis. Ignoring it, he was back behind the wheel, rolling down the road to where his eyes had shown him a strip of lights and the shaded structures of a town.

His teeth reflected off the moonlight as his stomach started to growl.

CHAPTER 5

Outside, the wind was blowing and packing leaves in the gutters, brushing the crowns of maples and shaking hedges and bushes. Her headlights cut the night like pale swords, and it was a dark one. Even with the moon out overhead, the night was solid as a well of shadows. Something was different about it. As if some intentional blackening had inked the sky, the spots between homes and pooled under cars; the hills that should be visible in the distance were rolling black lumps.

The neighborhood was quiet as usual, nothing about it had changed much, all but the pressing night that is. A couple was walking their small dog, pinching their coats against the wind. A few of the homes were dark, while most had the flare of lamplights on windows. Some of the driveways were empty, only a few cars were hanging against the curbs. Just another Friday night.

Oak Falls was nothing to write about it. Nothing that required the mind of an intellect or artist to paint. Its population was sparse but significant enough to require a full police force. Not that much happened out in Oak Falls, just your usual drunk driver, or petty thief. There were no armed robberies or murders in town, and rarely was there anything that required the hand of a detective to sift through. No, Oak Falls was a boring town, and its religion was football.

Jessica was never one to care much about football; could never understand what drove people to obsess about a silly oval made of pigskin. Her boyfriend, Jack, football was his life, his passion, his high school ball: his bible. Jessica's father loved football too, but her mother would rather knit blankets and read old paperbacks, mostly mysteries, some adventure. Maybe that's where she picked it up from, this disregard for football.

Brian, young Brian Berry, and his friends, Billy and Travis, were probably the only boys in town she knew that would rather play video games than throw a ball in the yard. She thought that was neat. She enjoyed babysitting him because he would always ask her to watch these crazy horror films with him. And he was sort of cute, a charmer. Too young for her, of course. But she always smiled about it. Jack, on the other hand, was an old-fashioned sort of man—took after his father—and sometimes that bothered her because it made her feel like she was something Jack could use when he wanted and wring out when he was finished with her. She knew he loved her, but sometimes she wanted to do other things than talk about football, hear about football, or watch him play football and sweat with his friends. Stephanie, her best friend, loved watching those men sweat, and her constant remarks about their physical abilities and what those muscles could do in bed, got to be redundant after a while. Stephanie was the sort that would take Jack if Jessica wasn't careful, so sometimes she had to keep an eye on her and her ear open.

But tonight wasn't about Stephanie or Jack, it was about Brian and his birthday. That's what mattered. She rented a few tapes from Gold Rush Video back in town. As she was browsing the shelves, she ran into Jack and some of his bulky friends. They spoke a little and he tried convincing her to drop the babysitting gig and come hang out with him at Bobby's party; told her it was going to be a big one and the whole team would be there. She asked if Stephanie was going to be there, because she hadn't heard from her all night, and he sort of blushed and disregarded the question, taking her in his big arms.

Jessica told him she had an obligation to the Berry's and couldn't be ditching them for a party. Besides, she was making thirty bucks off the gig, and she could use that to add to her savings.

Jack seemed angered over it, but retained his calm and kissed her on the cheek and told her he would maybe drop by a little later by the Berry's to have a little fun.

But, she wasn't in the mood for that. She wanted to have fun, yes, but not what he was after. She was tired and just wanted to relax and watch a few movies. A night like that was something Brian and his friends were always up for; they made the evenings fun. It made her feel weird at times to think things like that, being they were so young, but they were innocent, and she loved watching the movies they always seemed to watch.

While she checked out titles in the horror section, because that's what Brian preferred to watch, she picked two tapes she found appealing by the covers. One was titled: *The Dead Pit.* It involved a woman confined in a sanitarium, and she complained to the doctor about hearing voices of the dead speaking to her. Also, it starred some demonic doctor with red eyes that was raising a necrotic army out of a pit—or something like that.

The other flick had a man and woman on the cover; it also had this long, ghoulish shadow that was rising over the man. Called *Intruder,* it took place in a grocery store. In it, the staff is picked off one by one by some lunatic stalking the aisles and stockrooms. It sounded pretty good, she liked movies like that; she was pretty sure Brian would enjoy the movie too.

She felt bad that she hadn't bought him a gift, but as it was, her money was tight. Most of what she earned with these babysitting gigs of hers ended up in the bank or the tank. Jessica was trying her best to stack her funds so she could move out of town at some point. She wasn't the biggest fan of Oak Falls, but right now, she had to deal with it.

—

She swung a right on Brian's street. The houses down here were two-story models, all of them set back from one another at a good distance to keep privacy intact. There were plenty of big trees and bushes spotted around, and the lawns were green and well taken care of. His house was the furthest down the street, terminating at the end of a cul-de-sac that opened up onto a narrow creek with weeds and a thicket of oaks and cottonwoods, some maples.

Pulling up in the driveway, she eased the brake and shifted to park. She was gathering up her things while the radio continued to play at a low frequency. Consumed by grabbing her things, she was oblivious to the voice that cracked and interrupted the track that was playing.

In a stern voice, it said:

"*Attention, this is an alert from the California State Patrol. It has been learned that the notorious cannibal killer Kyle Cohen, known as Bones the Clown, responsible for a string of grisly crimes that took place in the late 70s to the early 1980s, has escaped Shady Sands Institute earlier today after having shot dead several of the staff and exiting the grounds on foot. Authorities are on high alert and enhancing their presence with patrols along the boundaries of Clemont, Rockton, and Oak Falls, all of which are in proximity to the aging hospital. We urge citizens to stay inside, and for whatever reason, do not answer—*"

Jessica shut the engine down, pocketed the keys, and stepped into the night.

—

Outside in the night and the wind, she felt small out there under the stars. The thing was, after she looked up in the black sky, she couldn't see much of the stars that normally popped in bright clusters over the town. The moon was in its rightful place, but something felt odd about it all. Not the moon, that is, but something—something sinister to the night. As if something was lurking around inside of it. She felt eyes on her coming from those oaks outside the Berry's property line. It was funny to her because she actually imagined something waiting for her in there. She couldn't explain it all that well, but it was tangible enough to put a chill up her backbone, and that was enough. She hurried to the stoop and rapped on the door. Vaguely, she could hear voices coming through the door from the other side. She was happy the lights were all on because being out there right then, in the wind and dark, it just—well, it just felt … *strange* to her.

The doorknob rattled, and Jessica jumped a little. She turned around, and looked at the field of oaks, at the black out there. Normally she would be able to see those hills rising and carpeted with clumps of trees and brush, but all she was seeing were sweeping shadows merging with a sky black as what was beneath it.

The door opened wide, and the sound of Brian

startled her with a small jump.

"Jessica! You're here!"

She smiled, feeling silly. "Happy Birthday, Brian!"

"Thank you—come inside—what do you got there?"

She flashed him the plastic containers that clasped over the movies. "A couple of horror films," she said in her best spooky voice.

Brian took them and read the titles. "Awesome! Thanks, Jess!"

Inside the house, the door sealed behind her, she ruffled her hair that had been tossed by the wind. She couldn't help but notice Brian staring at her like he always did. And who could blame him? She was wearing a soft blue shirt that dipped between her breasts a bit. A pair of faded jeans that formed to her legs as though the fabric was painted on. Her hair was an explosion of red curls, and her eyes, two green sparks.

"Is that Jessica?" a voice asked.

Jessica looked upstairs, at the banister, and saw Billy and Travis peeking between the wooden posts.

"Hey you guys, how is everyone?" she asked.

"We're good," Travis said, his face planted between the wood. "Now, we're even *better*."

"You know that sounded creepy, right?"

Brian glared up at Travis, narrowing his eyes.

"Did you bring the pizza?" Travis asked impatiently.

"Oh, shoot," she said, throwing her head back. "I totally forgot. I can go back real quick, it won't take me long."

"No, that's fine—we can order out," Brian told her.

"That's an idea. But it usually costs more that way, and I'm pretty light," she said, tapping at her pockets.

"Oh, that's okay, I got plenty of birthday money— I'll put that towards it."

"Are you sure?" she asked if maybe he shouldn't waste his money on pizza.

"Of course—hey, it's still *my* birthday, and a pretty girl like you needs something big and meaty with a lot of cheese on it—"

Billy and Travis laughed, their faces red behind the bars.

Jessica smiled, rouge on her cheeks.

"*Pizza*, I mean," Brian blushed, his hand slapping at his head.

"You're cute. Where should we order it from?"

"How about Pizza Hut?" Billy suggested, with his signature whiny voice. "They have great pizza."

"Pizza Hut is for people that don't understand good pizza," Travis countered. "I'm thinking … Round Table; they have this one—"

"It's my birthday, you idiot, so I'm choosing," Brian told him. He rubbed at his chin. "Oh—how about Crazy Clown Pizza?"

"Oh, I love that place," Billy said.

"Do they deliver?" Jessica asked.

Brian nodded. "Sure do, my parents ordered from there last week. It's so good. We have a magnet on the fridge. It's a big clown face eating a slice of pizza."

"That sounds good. Crazy Clown Pizza it is," she agreed.

"Are they better than Round Table?" Travis asked.

Brian gave him a thumbs up. "Anything is better than Round Table."

Travis looked offended. "You better be right, Berry—"

"Shut up."

Brian reached a hand out for Jessica's bag and the tapes she was holding. "Mind if I lighten that load for you, my lady?"

"Such a gentleman," she chuckled, handing him the tapes. "But I'll hold on to the bag."

"Hey Brian, do you want me to finish that level for you?" Billy asked, excited about the prospect of jumping back on Castlevania while Brian ogled Jessica.

"No, keep it paused. I'm *so* close to the boss, I want to beat it."

"Hey, *Brian*," Travis shouted, a sly grin on his lips. "Want me to show Jessica the present *I* got for you?"

Brian's face flooded red. "*No!* I mean—no, that's okay. She wouldn't like it."

"What did he get you?" Jessica asked, a pearly white grin on her face.

"Oh, just—some video game magazines, they're not the greatest though. Travis has bad taste."

"Actually, they're better than *video game* magazines, Jessica. They're—"

Brian reached out and curled Jessica's wrist,

dragging her further through the living room, avoiding the coffee table and couch, making a beeline for the kitchen. "We'll talk about it later— anyways, Jessica, we should order that pizza. They're probably pretty busy this Friday night."

"Yeah, you're right. Gold Rush was packed, you should have seen it. I ran into Jack while I was in there—"

Brian's momentum slowed. "He's not coming over here is he?"

She smiled at him. "No, he's actually going to be at a big party on the other side of town."

Brian furrowed his brow. "And you're not going with him?"

Again she smiled and ruffled his spiky hair. "I told him I had to watch my favorite person tonight."

Brian blushed.

"What did he say?"

"He was pretty mad about it. But I told him I would hang out with him another time. I also told him it was your birthday today and we were going to watch movies tonight."

Brian felt good about it. "Did you tell him anything else?"

"Like what?"

"Uh … nothing, I guess."

"You're too cute, Brian. You're the little brother I never had."

Brian's heart nearly split. "Your *brother*?"

"Of course—" she put those fiery green eyes on him and swiped at a curl of red hooking her brow "—

the greatest brother." She leaned in and kissed him on the cheek.

Travis and Billy made noises that sounded like lips smacking and Brian blushed. "Uh, I gotta go, Jess, I'll be right back though—phone is over there, and the number is on the fridge—"

He said something else but Jessica couldn't hear him. He was already upstairs by the time she reached for the phone.

CHAPTER 6

He ditched the truck back up the road in a copse of trees; made sure to conceal it good enough so it wouldn't be found before he had his fun. He knew the cops would be out in force now, considering he reduced two of them into something slick enough to run a hose over. Since his escape, he had felt an ever-growing need to eat. That man's heart back there, it wasn't enough. It lacked the pure quality a young boy or girl had in it. The heart of the man was old and had issues; it was bitter—but it did the job—for now.

Bones ditched the hospital garb, preferring to stalk the woods in the flesh. Still armed with the pistol and the knife, he kept to the shade of the trees, which wasn't hard on account the night was a pressed blackness that made seeing a hand in front of your face a near impossible thing. But Bones was pale, his body hadn't felt the touch of the sun in years. Even when he was allowed freedom in the yard of the Institute—which was very brief—he was chained to a tree, and usually was companioned by a guard who had a gun resting on him the whole time.

With his pale complexion, he could very well be picked out by an observant eye. It was only a matter of time before the police took to the sky and hit these hills with spotlights.

He had to be careful.

—

It was the sound of an engine that brought him to a stop. He tracked the gears through the trees. He couldn't see much beyond the black walls around him, but the sound was enough to follow. He started in the direction he felt it was coming from, and after crossing what had to be a hundred meters of black flooded woods, his eyes detected the sparks of lights. Natural lights, like something a home would give off.

Keeping low, he moved, his senses firing and his eyes wide, homing in on the needles of light. Another fifty feet and the trees thinned in narrow gaps, and he saw the distinct outline of a home—a few homes. But one grabbed him. It was the one with the car idling outside in the driveway. Being so black outside, he couldn't see the person in it—or if there were a person in it at all. But it was rumbling, the headlights were splashing the garage door.

Suddenly, the engine went silent and the lights winked out.

A door screeched open and slammed just as quickly. He heard footsteps smacking the pavement of a walkway and then he was able to verify the red, curly hair and slender body in the light of the home.

She was young, and that's all that mattered. Even at the distance that separated her from him, Bones could smell her; could smell something coming off of her. Maybe it was that warm spot between her legs. The wind was blowing harder and all that lotion on her body and in her hair was blowing against him and it put his cock to a rigid pole. He edged the skin of it with the knife, just enough to draw a seam of blood down the center.

From the house, she looked into the trees, and Bones watched her. He knew she couldn't see him. It was too black where he was; he was in the heart of the shadows; he was a shadow; a lurking phantom of the woods; a witch; a night demon; the claws in the closet and the winging shape against the moon. That was Bones. And he was looking right at her with that face of his that looked more like the skull of a scarecrow and a mouth crammed with spiky teeth.

She must have felt him somehow. Felt something watching her; he could sense it alright. He had seen many young people watch those dark places between buildings; or hollows between trees; he had seen the hesitancy in the young boy's eyes as he stood at the top of the stairs leading down into the cellar. That boy's friends had dared him to go in there with taunts and shoves. Oh yes, they dared him and he went on down there, his body shaking the whole time. Because he knew, he knew what was waiting down there for him in the dark—maybe it wasn't Bones the Clown waiting on him—but it was something gnarled and withered and crooked with big claws hooked to rend; something with irradiated yellow eyes. The boy screamed when all those terrors in his mind were no longer figments, but whole and complete; and when he saw Bones shambling after him with that hatchet in his fist, that clown costume, that face paint, all he could do was piss himself and scream as the blade unzipped his throat.

The kids upstairs weren't laughing at him anymore, because they all felt it. Each of those boys felt something pernicious stewing down in those black shadows. It was like staring down into an open grave, waiting for something to reach out at them and take them down there with it.

Bones tossed them a gift from below. It landed on the wall behind them with a wet smack. And once the kids watched that brain slide down the wall like a clump of bloody snot, they ran away like a bunch of agitated bats off a cave ceiling, screaming.

Yes, Bones had experienced many occasions like that, and he was looking forward to another moment to reminisce on. He was looking to better acquaint himself with that girl out there too, that was something he needed to do.

Her demeanor changed, and Bones heard something else—smelled something else. It was the sound of children. A boy. Not too young, but not too old—just right, according to the wind.

He licked the knife clean with a long red tongue, and as the girl went into the house and the door slammed hard behind her, Bones left behind the umbral canopy of the trees and loped forward across the green acre—just a hunched, pale stick-figure of a nightmare.

CHAPTER 7

The man was screaming, screaming as though he were emptying his lungs to fill the back of the room. His legs were shaking and his arms were fidgeting, but the man holding him down wouldn't release his hold.

The meat saw was inching closer, its vibrations shook the plate pressed against his cheek. The man's screams became unbearable, almost decibel breaking. His eyes widened as the thin blade neared. It was through his cheeks in the next blink, and its teeth chewed through his face like a flame through wax, shredding sinew into gristle, and shaving bone; running through his teeth and separating his skull. His body flopped—

"Holy shit, that was crazy!" Travis shouted.

Brian nodded. "I've never seen anything like that —it looked so real."

"I don't know how they do that, but I want to learn!" Billy said excitedly. "Did you see those teeth? The way the saw hit them and they popped from his gums like that?"

"Ugh," Jessica shivered. "That was pretty gross,

Billy; I can still see it."

Brian leaned forward off the couch and grabbed his Pepsi. It left a wet ring on the coffee table. Cushioning his back against the cream fabric of the sofa, he took a pull and looked over to Jessica who was seated next to him, her legs crossed, her chest lifted, her face twisted in concentration. Twice already had she ducked her head toward his shoulder, her hand covering her face. That felt good. And when she did it, he could smell her perfume; it was a light vanilla scent, and it smelled good. Brian couldn't get enough of it. He loved when she watched horror movies with them because she always did these things. He couldn't wait until the day he was old enough to make a move on her. Being young when the girl you wanted was eighteen and had an asshole for a boyfriend just wasn't fair; that was life though he supposed.

"How you liking *Intruder*, Jess?" he asked her.

"It's pretty scary," she said, her eyes on the screen.

"Yeah, it's a good one so far. I'm still wondering who the killer is."

"It's the boyfriend, you dufus," Travis said, a can of Sprite in his hand.

"Nah, that's too obvious," countered Billy. "It's probably that guy who she has a crush on."

"That's what I'm thinking," Brian said, placing his Pepsi back on the table. "Or, the owner. Who do you think it is, Jess?"

She pressed her lips out, her eyes narrowed, her mind engaging. "I dunno—oh, maybe the other guy;

the other owner."

"What?" Travis laughed. "No way—it's definitely not him."

"Why do you say that?" she asked him.

"Because he loves that place; loves those people; he wouldn't do that. I'm telling you all, it's her ex-boyfriend."

The doorbell rang.

"I'll get it—pause the movie," Brian said.

The money was on the table. He scooped it up and counted it as he walked through the living room into the foyer. Throwing the chain back on the door, unlatching the bolt, he swung it open.

A clown was standing there. A tall clown in a white and black jumper. He had a big red afro and a big red nose. There was something big in his hand, and he was holding it out for Brian.

"Crazy Clown Pizza," the clown said. "The damage is $13.25."

"Awesome costume, man," Brian told him with a smirk. "Here's fifteen—you can keep the change."

The clown handed over the pizza. "Thanks, little man. Enjoy!"

"Yeah, you too—" *Damn*, Brian thought, *why do I always say that?*

"Was that the pizza guy?" Travis shouted from the living room.

Brian walked in, holding the square box to his nose. "It smells so good—to the dining room!"

"Why there? Why can't we eat it right here?"

"Because, if you or Billy get tomato sauce on the

couch, or anywhere else, my parents will *kill* me."

"What if Jessica got sauce on the couch?"

Jessica smiled at Brian. He smiled back. How could he ever deny her anything?

"She wouldn't. She's not a *Neanderthal* like you."

Billy laughed.

"It's not a big deal T, we can still watch the movie if we all sit near the end of the table."

"Or we can all eat and talk," Jessica suggested. "The movie isn't going anywhere."

"Good idea, Jess," Brian agreed.

"Oh great, what are we going to talk about?" Travis asked.

Brian thought about it as he placed the pizza box on the dining table, and lifted the top back. The smell of the pizza filled the room. It was pepperoni and sausage, heavy on the cheese. It pooled in the center and each slice was lost in a thick lake of cheese and meat. "We can talk about the movie."

"You guys are too much," Jessica chuckled, taking down some plates from the cabinet. "Anybody want a fork—anything?" she called from the kitchen.

"Who eats pizza with a fork?" Travis asked, perplexed by the notion.

Jessica grabbed one for herself. "Those of us who are further up the evolutionary chain."

Billy laughed. Brian seized the moment. "I'll take one too, Jess."

Travis was flustered, but let it pass. "Well, whatever, I just want to get back to the movie. It's too good. I wonder what *The Dead Pit* is like."

"Looks like it's about zombies or something; at least by the cover it does," Billy said, reaching for a slice of pizza. "Dang, we might need a pizza cutter for this pie."

"Oh, I'm totally ready to watch a zombie movie," Travis said as he reached across the table for a plate. "Besides, the girl on the back of the box is pretty hot. Wouldn't you agree, Bri?"

Brian shook his head, noticed Jessica watching him. "Uh ... yeah, she's alright, I guess."

Travis sat down, scooting closer to the table. "Kind of like those mag—"

"So, Jessica—" Brian quickly interrupted.

She was reaching for the pizza and stopped. "Yes?"

"Um ... what—what do you think of—it's pretty windy outside, right?"

Travis laughed.

Brian reddened.

"What's so funny?" Jessica asked.

Brian stared at Travis like he wanted to smack him. "It's nothing—Travis is just weird."

She narrowed her eyes, her lips curling. She shook her head and red curls shook with it. "You guys."

CHAPTER 8

As the wind blew against him, ruffling the silky clown jumper, out of the corner of his eye he thought he detected something, something like white limbs against the black night, and for a moment there, it sounded vaguely like somebody was running up on him. But as he turned with anticipation to greet whatever it was, there was nothing there, nothing but the big house, some trees shaking in the wind, bushes leaning against drafts, leaves skittering. A dog barked somewhere distant. Folding the money over in his hand, he pocketed it, reached for the handle of his car, and stopped.

This time, it was something else. He turned rather quickly, certain he heard somebody laughing at him. But the laugh was all wrong, it was like listening to one of those old Halloween spook tracks with the cackling monster; it had that same horrible frequency, dense and overlaying with static. It almost sounded like it was in his head, or something carried by the wind. It was hard to describe, but he felt it all the same.

Shrugging, he swung the door open on his Dart

and paused. In the road, not five feet from the hood of his car was a man. But this was no ordinary person; nobody stable would be out in this darkness and wind and naked. But it wasn't the lack of clothes that disturbed Tony so much as it was the way the man looked; his complexion, that narrow face, and eyes, dark like the hollows of a skull. He was grinning, or what could be considered a grin. It was something like a jackal would grin if it could exaggerate such a thing. The silky clown jumper shifted with the wind some more and Tony felt those eyes searching over him. A tremor coiled his body and a chill iced his skin.

"You okay there?" Tony asked this naked man, almost afraid to do so. "Do you need help?"

Something wasn't right here, that much he felt the moment he saw the man, and right away, Tony, with instinctive regard for assistance, looked behind him, hoping to see someone familiar, someone that could help him with this obviously confused—and frightening looking—person. But when he looked back at the man, there was nothing there.

Tony tensed, half expecting to have that man jump out at him, wrap him in his arms and strangle him or do something worse. Tony checked all around him, narrowed his glare to every angle; to each cleft of shadow, to those black wooded hills, but there was nothing. It was almost like he had imagined it the way you sometimes see things out of the corner of your eye, and when you go to confront that leering object sitting there, there's an empty space, just a figment of something playing a trick on you. It felt intangible, like a ghost. Considering the man's body was sickly pale and lacking weight, he had the effulgent frame of a specter, and that theory spooked him. A chill ran through him, and Tony ducked into his car, keyed the ignition in a hurry, turned the headlights on—

And that's when he saw him. Captured in the low beams of the square lights: the naked man. But he wasn't standing there waiting for an invitation, he was coming at Tony.

Tony shouted in disgust, in revulsion at the shambling strides of the man. He was like a galloping, pale spider, with a wide revolting grin slashed on his face, and something in his hand.

Before Tony could react in time, Bones was on the man. Leaning into the car, his arm shot out and the knife point punched a narrow slot in Tony's head, transfixing his skull. His body convulsed as the blade poisoned his mind, and blood poured from his eyes, and drained from his nose in two thick red threads. His eyes boiled over white as his mouth opened and closed in suffocating gasps as his lungs tried swallowing air. Slowly his body settled down in death.

Bones ejected the blade and its extraction was a sickening suction sound. He brought its red-stained surface to his face and ran his tongue up and along its length. It tasted good but lacked the purity of young blood.

Leaning forward into the car, he grabbed the

body under the shoulders and dragged it out onto the road. There, he turned it over and hurriedly removed the costume.

Call it luck or fate, but to Bones, it was a sign.

Here was a man he killed who was wearing a clown costume. The shoes were normal sneakers, so he would have to go barefoot, which would aid him considerably in his stealth. But the costume, the very image of its material, the feel of it between his fingers, and now pressed to his flesh, it imbibed him with a strength he hadn't felt in years. New confidence surged in his blood. Though he lacked the paint, the black and white jumper was sufficient, and with it, he had been resurrected. A celebration would begin. A great feast.

Yes, he would eat well and fuck hard and slay many!

But, first, he had to hide this body.

CHAPTER 9

"No, I can't leave, I have to watch Brian. How would it look if I—"

"I'm trying to be nice about it, Jess, but you're making that hard. I'm asking you to please just stop by for a little bit, and after, you can leave and go back and watch those little brats."

Jessica was already sick of the conversation. After they finished the pizza and watched the ending of *Intruder*—which was incredible—Jack had been pestering the Berry household with phone calls every five minutes. The first one or two were fine, but after the fifth, and now the seventh, it was getting out of hand. And, Jack was drunk; and when he got drunk, he started slurring his words and releasing long dormant thoughts in his mind. It came out in a poisonous string of hurtful things she was honestly getting tired of hearing. He started in on how Stephanie was here at the party and she was having a good time and they were talking about the game last week, and some other things. Stephanie asked Jack if he could drive her home after the party too; implying things that he would like to do to

Stephanie because she had the time to spend with him and Jessica's time was always wasted working and saving money, doing babysitting gigs on the side. It was getting to be a burden with Jack, and he let her know that in his inebriated state.

"I'm having a good time here, Jack. I'll talk to you tomorrow—"

"Just give me a minute, okay? Is that too much to ask for your boyfriend? I don't understand what it is about you Jessica that you feel the need to give me the cold shoulder every now and then—like I did something to you. What wrong is there in wanting my girlfriend by my side?"

"Nothing," she said weakly. "I'm just not up for it. I'm tired and I have obligations."

That got him mad. "Your obligations are to me! I'm important—I'm the one that is going to marry you, and if you can't see that, then maybe I figured you out wrong. Your little friend over here has time for me—time to spend talking to me about the game and my prospects for State. Why can't you fucking talk to me about shit like that? Why is it always—"

"Then talk to her!" Jessica slammed the phone.

She wiped a tear from her cheek and ran her fingers under her sockets. She was staring out the kitchen window, out into the yard. She could see the grass lit up by the porch light. Beyond that was dark and seamed in blackness. The wind was carrying leaves across the grass.

"Brian," she called over her shoulder, stifling her scratchy throat. They were still watching *The Dead*

Pit, all gathered in the living room. "I'm going out back to clear my head a minute. I'll be right back."

"Okay, Jess!" Brian shouted.

She stepped outside and was immediately swept by a gust. It felt good, the coolness of it, the relief of it. Sitting there on the porch, she leaned back, her hands smoothed on the maple deck, her red hair dripping behind her as she faced the sky. It was still stained with that ebony screen. She couldn't see many stars, and she wondered why. The moon had drifted and was sitting over the black hills. She thought about Jack, and what he could be doing. What Stephanie was doing. She had a thought that maybe they were making out right now in Jack's truck, beneath this awful inked sky. Could be that she was straddling him right now, her panties rubbing against the bulge in his jeans. She imagined her hand on his cock and stroking it, maybe it was in her mouth, in her pussy, maybe her ass. It was all the things Jessica did for him. But it was never enough. She caught him with three girls in the past. In each case they were doing something with one another, stuff she didn't like seeing him do to other girls. And he enjoyed it judging by that look on his face.

Why didn't she just leave? It was a question she asked herself often. But she loved him. They had been together three years and she lost herself to him; he promised he loved her.

It was all too much.

"You okay out there?" A muffled voice asked from behind.

She twisted and saw Brian's face pressed between the curtains of the square window in the kitchen door. She smiled. "Yeah, just need a breather."

"You need any company?" he asked.

She wiped a string of red hair out of her eyes. "Thank you, Brian, but I want to be alone right now."

"Okay, but hurry up, you're missing an awesome movie!"

She laughed. Brian had the traits she wished Jack had. It made her feel awful—a bit nasty—thinking about it. He was a young boy, just turned twelve. But the qualities he had; his quarks, it's what she wanted Jack to have. Jack was the opposite. He was brash and full of himself. An ego that increased with each yard he ran. When the cheerleaders screamed his name, his dick got hard and that ego kept rising. She figured she only fell for him for superficial reasons. He was handsome and strong; blue eyes, a strong face, short blond hair, and wide shoulders. But, it was a mistake, and now torn by her emotions for him, she had a weight pressing against her, and it was starting to crush her.

Sighing, she stood and stretched, and stared off into the yard. It was a big yard, two big maples were reaching overhead, a tool shed further back, but she couldn't see much of that. She turned to go back into the house, but there was a glimpse of something in her eye. It was like a faint line of silver, a flash of something. She kept her eyes on the spot, but nothing else showed. *Could have been a trick of the eye*, she thought. But, *wait*, she thought again.

She took a step down onto the yard, the grass cushioned against her bare feet. Watching the dark, there was a distinction to it. It was an outline, like something carved and emerging, detached from its bold surface. It was illusory, like a three-dimensional figure popping out at you. As she kept staring at it, it began to manifest with contours, edging through the black.

She gasped.

It was a man. That's what she was thinking; that's what it looked like to her. But, she couldn't see him all that well in the night. Feeling the wind blowing into her, she jumped back onto the deck, and without looking back, hurried quickly into the house.

CHAPTER 10

She came through the kitchen like a wind, eyes widened, almost a shocked sort of look that people get after getting spooked about something.

"What is it, Jess?" Brian asked leaning forward off the couch, detecting the change in her. "Are you okay?"

"Yeah, Jess, you like you seen a ghost," Travis added.

Jessica shook her head. "No, I—I think I might have seen somebody—outside—in your backyard."

Brian stood up, grabbed the remote, and paused the movie. "A person? In my yard?"

"I think." Jessica ran her fingers through her hair and picked a leaf out of her curls. "It looked like a person."

Brian started for the kitchen. Casually, he walked across the mocha-shaded tiles. Pushing aside the flower-patterned curtains, he squinted, searching the blackness for something that resembled a man.

"I'm not seeing anything," he said after a moment.

"I saw it, Brian," she said, curling her fingers into

her palms. "It's out there, next to where your father's tool shed is at."

He looked again. "Hmm," he shrugged. "Not seeing anything. It's really dark out there though."

"What did you see exactly, Jess?" Billy asked her.

"I was looking out into the yard, and I swear I saw something move. And I watched it to make sure, and then ... well it took the shape of a person—I think."

"Well, was it a person or maybe a bush?"

"I know what a *person* looks like, Travis," she said, her voice rising.

"Okay, okay, but—" Travis split the blinds on the picture window looking out into the yard. "Was it a man or a woman?"

"I—" she hesitated. She couldn't say what it was. She hadn't seen it all that well. Just that vague, silhouette of a person, but ... there was something about it. Rising from it like a vapor. But placing that feeling into a category that made sense to describe, was difficult because she was unable to find the words. She felt uneasy about the figure. Like the feeling you would get staring at a wild animal out in the woods. The freedom a mountain cat would have to leap on you and gnaw your bones down to brittle twigs. It was that feeling. But how could she explain that without sounding stupid?

"I couldn't tell."

Travis rolled his eyes.

"It *was* a person, Travis. I know it was. And something about them—well, it freaked me out. I don't know—"

"It's okay, Jessica," Brian said calmly. "Why don't we get some flashlights—my dad has some in the garage—and go out and take a look."

"I don't think that's a good idea," she said.

"Why not?" Travis asked.

"Because who knows what kind of weirdo is out there?"

"Jess—" Travis laughed "—if you haven't forgotten already, Oak Falls is as innocent as a newly born lamb. The only weirdos out here are your boyfriend and his stupid jock friends."

"I dunno—"

"Look, Jess," Brian started. "We'll just stay on the deck, and search the backyard with our flashlights. If we see somebody, we'll come back inside and call the police or something. Sound good?"

She bit her lip. "Okay, but just for a minute."

—

They came out of the garage with two flashlights —it was all they could find. One was a big silver-handled model, the end as wide as a tea saucer. The other was a green plastic one with a short handle and a weak beam. Brian took the heavier one while Travis had the other. Billy brought a chisel along with him. He told Brian, Just in case.

Jessica thought it was a bad idea. She was supposed to be watching and taking care of these kids, not encouraging them into harm. What if something bad happened to them? She would feel wrecked, absolutely awful about it.

Brian swung the back door open, and the wind pushed against it. "Getting cold out there," he said, a hint of nervous strain in his voice. But he couldn't be nervous. He was the man of the house after all. He was twelve today, and he had to show Jessica there was nothing to be afraid of. So she saw a person, big deal. It could have been that asshole boyfriend of hers. Or, just imagination. The dark played tricks on the eyes and peopled shadows with things that made you cry out, thinking you had seen an image that was never there. Regardless if there was a person outside his home, he would face it with courage, not unease.

They stepped onto the deck and instantly the wind played against them. The maples were thrashing and he could hear what sounded like his father's tool shed door creaking. That was funny because his father never left it unlocked, and if he had, he would have made sure to shut the door. His dad was like that. He was a neat freak and kept order with things but in a good and decent way.

"Sounds like something banging out there," Billy said, his fingers tightening on the chisel.

"Yeah Bri, sounds like your dad's tool shed."

Brian nodded. "That's what I'm thinking too. But —" he popped the light and its wide beam cleaved open the black. "Dang, I can't see that far."

"Did your dad leave it open?" Jessica asked, shouldered beside Brian.

"No, he never leaves it open. Hmm, where did you see this person?"

She pointed to a spot between the maples about forty feet away. "In between there."

Brian swung the light in there, its path burned into the shadows and chased them back far enough for him to see the trunks of the maples, a little bit of the shed. "Not seeing anything—"

"Brian—" Travis shouted "—over there!"

They all followed the beam of his light.

Billy sounded jumpy. "What—what do you see?"

"Oh," Travis gasped, holding his stomach. "It's just my shadow."

Brian punched and shoved him. "*Not* funny, man, you scared the hell out of me for a minute."

"*Definitely* not funny, Travis," Jessica stated in something like a mom voice.

"Oh, calm down you guys, I was just lightening up the mood."

"Well, it wasn't funny," Brian said.

Billy saw it. Yeah, he saw it alright. He saw that man over there peeking out at him from behind the tree while the rest of his friends were arguing about Travis' trick. He couldn't see much, but he saw the face, and what there was of it, looked too much like something you would imagine rising out of the grave and groaning for blood. The chisel dropped from his hand.

Brian turned at the sound, swinging his light down on the tool. "Be careful man, my dad sees a scrape in his deck he'll blame me and I'll get in a lot of trouble."

Billy picked it up but didn't say anything.

Brian had his light up under Billy's face. "You okay, there, Billy?"

Billy nodded.

"You sure?"

Billy looked up and pointed to the yard. "I saw it, Brian—there was a person out there, over by the trees."

Both flashlights peeled back the night, their blades fusing. The width was a pool of spotlight that showered over the yard, but couldn't find anything.

"I'm not seeing anything, Billy," Brian said.

"There's nothing out there," Travis said, sure of himself.

"Yeah, because whoever that was went back behind the tree—I'm telling you I saw a face."

"I don't like this you guys, let's get back inside," Jessica told them.

"Just a minute—" Travis trailed off the deck, walking through the grass "—I want to check it out."

"Are you fucking nuts?" Jessica asked him.

"*Whoa*," Travis said. "That was new, Jess. I'll only be a minute, don't get your panties in a knot."

"No Travis," Brian said, his voice rising and stern. "If Billy says he saw somebody and Jessica swear she did too, then I think somebody is probably out there. And since they're not saying anything or showing themselves, maybe we should go back inside and call somebody."

"I know you're trying to impress your girlfriend, Brian, but I think it'll be okay if I go and check it out." Travis walked on over there, unfaded by the words ringing out from his friends on the deck. His light blade jumped over the grass. Coming up to the maple, he tip-toed as he got closer, looked back to his friends, put his finger to his mouth, jumped behind the tree, and said: "Surprise!"

But then something had him and he was pulled behind the tree.

Jessica screamed, and Billy did too. Brian flashed his light on the tree—all three were screaming.

"*Travis!*"

And that's when they saw him. Travis. He came out, laughing, and bent over in chuckles, his flashlight waving at them. "Man, you guys—you should see your faces from here. You really believed it!"

"That is *not* fucking funny!" Jessica stammered.

"You're an *asshole*," Brian told him.

"Dude, my heart," Billy said holding his chest.

Travis was still laughing, still bent over, wheeling his flashlight.

The phone rang in the house, and Jessica screamed at the sound.

"Shit!" she said. "That scared me. I'm going inside; I've had enough of this."

Brian kept his light pinned on Travis. "You sure there's nothing out there?"

Travis only kept laughing. "There's nothing out here, Brian. She was seeing things!"

The door whacked inside the kitchen hard after catching some wind. The phone was still ringing. "Well, I'm going in then you asshole!" He stopped to look at Billy. "You coming?"

Billy only stood there, inert and being brushed with the wind. He knew what he saw. But was it real? Maybe he didn't see it. Maybe it was all because of the movie? Who really knew? Either way, if Travis was out there, saying there was nothing out there, then maybe Billy was just seeing things. But something bothered him. If Jessica said—*swore*—she saw a person, and he saw what looked like a face, doesn't that validate that there was, or is, indeed someone out there? Perhaps they ran away; jumped the fence once they saw Travis coming toward them.

"Yeah, I'm coming," he finally said.

Brian and Billy stepped inside the home, the door still opened behind them.

Travis had himself a laugh and he loved it. The faces on them, he thought. They're all so stupid!

He started back to the house when a hand reached out from behind him and clamped his mouth. He fell back into something rustling, like a silk sheet. He dropped the light and grabbed at the fingers, but those fingers were incredibly strong like steel cables, and he couldn't pry them loose. Something sharp poked his back, and his eyes widened as whatever it was sunk into him. His legs reacted and started winging and wheeling as he was lifted off the grass. He was being hauled back further into the shadows of the yard.

Bones the Clown released his hold on the boy's mouth, but was quick enough to reach inside that mouth with a pair of prune trimmers and cut out the tongue before he could scream. Travis' eyes nearly burst at the pain as blood flooded over his face. He was hurled to the ground hard, and as he looked up, he got a look at the man hovering over him. It was a clown, an honest-to-God clown. But this clown was something you would see chasing after you through a boneyard of a carnival in a nightmare. It was a ghoulish parody of a clown. The clown's face was shallow and dimpled and sickly, like a skull. As Travis kicked and spit blood, the clown was busy bringing something else out. It took a moment for Travis to see it in the dark, but then he saw the tiny metal teeth of the tool and knew it was a wood saw of some type. It had a short blade with a thick oak handle, and it fell over Travis' face in a razored line. The clown made something like a laugh from its throat, and the tiny teeth of the saw began thrashing into Travis' face.

The pain was unbearable. Blood was filling his eyes and he wanted to scream, but with the saw grinding through his mouth and chipping his teeth, all he could do was grunt and whine and gargle the blood filling his throat.

The edge of the saw shaved through the skull and Travis' world went black. His life was gone in a flash as the tiny teeth ate into the meat of his brain.

Finished with his work, Bones the Clown peeled the boy's head apart with his hands. Webs of blood tethered the halves like guts in a pumpkin. He pushed the strings aside and grabbed a fistful of brain. It was hot and juices were running down his fingers and coming together at the back of his hand. He placed it in his mouth. His teeth pulped the clump of brain like a juicy plum. Blood and fluids streaked his chin.

It was perfect. It tasted young and pure, everything he was waiting for. Yes, this was good, and he would eat some more. Greedily, his fingers clawed at the boy's skull until he emptied it of its meat. From the shadows of the yard, he looked to the house, a bloody wide grin on his face.

So much more meat. Children meat.

CHAPTER 11

"Who's on the phone?" Brian asked her.

She put a finger in the air to quiet him; her focus on the phone. "No, he left here awhile ago. Well, yes, I can check." She put the phone on her shoulder and asked if Brian could check out the window and tell her if he sees a car outside on the curb. She told him it would have a big clown head magnetized to the top. Brian came back a second later, a strange look on his face.

"What is it, Brian?"

"It's still outside—the car's on the curb."

Her mouth dried up. "Actually, my little brother told me he sees the car outside on the curb."

Billy was seated at the table, staring at the back door in the kitchen. It was still standing open, the wind was causing it to shake.

"I'm not going outside," she told the other man on the line. She said a few more things, but then Billy brought up the absence of Travis, and the room became silent.

Brian searched the living room like Travis had come inside without him noticing. "He's not in the house?"

Billy shook his head. "I never saw him come in. He was still laughing out there in the yard."

Brian poked his head out the door. "Travis!"

Nothing but the wind in reply.

"Hold on," Jessica told the person on the phone. She looked at Brian. "Where's Travis?"

Brian pointed at the door. "He never came in. I bet he's playing another joke on us." He shut the door and locked it, laughing. "Let's see him think how funny it is when I lock him outside and don't let him all night."

"Don't do that, Brian," Jessica told him.

There was a tapping at the window, and it spooked Billy so bad he about leaped up out of the chair he was seated in. "Did you hear that?" he asked.

"Hear what?" Brian said, drawing the chain in the slot of the door.

"I—I heard a tapping—right there on the window."

"A tapping?"

"Yeah, like fingers drumming on the glass."

Jessica was talking to the person on the phone, letting them know they thought that they might have seen a man in their backyard, and the car of their employee was empty but suggested that maybe he was visiting someone in the neighborhood, and this wasn't their problem. She was trying to listen to both the stressed out employee of the pizza place, and the conversation that Billy and Brian were sharing.

"Yep, I bet it's Travis too. That asshole." Brian peeled the blinds open. "It's too dark."

There was a knock on the kitchen door.

Brian froze, as did Billy, and Jessica.

There was something different about that knock. It was the sound of a heavy fist, nothing like Travis' fist, but had the weight of an adult. It knocked again, and Brian was threaded with a crawling feeling.

"That can't be Travis," he said, his voice hollow, the air in the kitchen thinned and replaced with an inching dread.

"Well, then who the hell is it?" Billy asked, his usually whiny voice now more of a loud whisper.

Brian kept his voice low. "Maybe it's that pizza delivery man. Maybe he's weird and messing with us. It would make sense. Some of the people that work there are scary looking."

Jessica was overcome with a feeling that was making her heart leap. The air was drying up in her lungs and she felt some impending terror in the air. It was instincts, primal and honed through eons of survival. And right then, it was standing out, making itself known in her, and peeling open her mind with all sorts of speculation.

She went to say something to the man on the phone, but she hadn't gotten out two words when the picture window in the dining room shattered and the blinds thrashed aside as a body came crashing through, landing with a sick splatter on the table. Blood showered the walls and ceiling and sprayed Billy in the face. All three started screaming as their eyes widened in shock at the mutilated corpse of Travis, his skull cracked open and gutted.

And framed behind it, behind the twisted mess of the blinds, oily with blood, was a clown.

CHAPTER 12

"Damn," the man said, holding the phone away from his ear. He cradled the phone and looked over at Dean, the manager. "That was weird."

Dean stood there with his hands on his hips, a baggy clown outfit hanging off of him. "Well, are you going to keep me in suspense or what, Rick?"

Rick looked at the phone like something was wrong with it. "I—well, there was screaming; the lady said clown real loud. I heard some kids' voices too. But …"

"Spit it out, Rick!"

"Well, there was a laugh."

"A laugh?" Dean said impatiently "What the hell are you talking about?"

"It sounded like a laugh, but weird; there must be a crossed line or something because it sounded like two or three people laughing at the same time. I dunno."

Rick continued to stare at the phone on the wall.

"So, what about Tony?"

"Well, the lady said something about a clown, maybe—no—I don't know what to tell you, Dean, but that was pretty freaky."

"Freaky? Rick, where the fuck is Dean at? I need him here. I have deliveries hanging out of my ass!"

"Dean, I have a bad feeling."

Dean laughed. "What's the matter with you?"

"That laugh, Dean! And, their voices, their *screams*. It wasn't right, man. It sounded real; like they were really terrified. I heard a bunch of glass breaking and—"

"Fucking goddamn Tony—it's him again. He always does this shit!"

Rick was confused. "*Does* what?"

"Fuck around. One time, he didn't come back for two hours! Two fucking hours that I was paying the sonofabitch and he couldn't even answer the goddamn phone at his house. You know what he told me when he returned to work after that?"

Rick nodded.

"He said he forgot where we were located," Dean laughed. "Can you believe that shit?"

"Dean, this—this was different. I'm telling you right now, I have a bad feeling." Rick plucked the phone up.

"What the hell you doing?" Dean asked.

"I'm calling the police."

"The police?" Dean said as if that was the stupidest shit he'd ever heard. "What the hell for?"

"I told you, it was really weird sounding. I think they're in trouble."

"Oh, that's bullshit! They're probably playing a prank on you."

"No, I don't think so."

"Fuck it—you want to call the cops, then you call them, and you tell them to slap those cuffs on Tony for being such a fucking hemorrhoid." Dean marched off, wringing his arms in the air.

Rick called the cops and told him what he heard. Gave them the address to the last place Tony delivered. They informed him that they would let him know what happened when they figured it out.

CHAPTER 13

Jessica moved faster than she herself thought was possible. She hooked both Brian and Billy on the back of the neck and hauled them upstairs, slammed the door behind her, wrenched the lock, and had both boys help her push a dresser against it. They barricaded themselves in the parent's room. Brian said they had a phone in here and went to grab it. The moment he brought it out of its cradle, the line went dead, and so did the lights. Plunged in black, they waited.

—

It was around five minutes ago that Travis' body landed on the table, but felt like hours. During that time, all she could hear was shallow breathing and heartbeats, the sound of pain squeezing out tears, and small children crying and whimpering, unable to keep their sobs from being hoarse. It was sad and unnerving; also frightening. Her heart felt as though it were ready to grow hands and claw its way from her breast and dive out the window. None of them had said a word once the dresser was secured behind the door. Words were hard to come by without shaking and thinking of that man they saw outside; no, not a *man*, but a *clown*. Not a silly, colorful clown with a big spotted bow tie and rainbow cotton hair, a balloon animal blowing from his lips. This was something *like* a clown. A perversion; a configuration of both ghoul and clown and madman—a grim combination that showed itself in the clown's face. It was a pitted, eroded-looking mask of flesh, white as the moon. The eyes were the worse, yawing black like two open graves. Jessica imagined worms inside those pits, but nothing like that was there, because this thing wasn't dead, but *alive*. It was alive and standing out that window when she saw it, something like a grin on its face that looked more like a knife had peeled the skin around its teeth away. She saw the teeth too, all in that split second before she grabbed the boy's and raced out of there. Those teeth were pointed like a shark's teeth. They were red too like he was eating meat and drinking blood, which, for some reason, she had a feeling that he *was*. And poor Travis, laying there like something offered to a ghoulish family on Thanksgiving. It made her stomach curl up in a ball of nausea.

Jessica wondered what had happened to that clown. Did he enter the house? Or was he still outside, ringing the property like some rabid animal about to leap on its prey? She could picture it that way, but she was also picturing other things. Horrible things. Like that clown's shadow going up the stairs growing longer with each step and his shark teeth red and glowing, and something curved in his fist, the edge seamed in meat and blood.

That's what I saw outside from before, she thought. *I saw him out there, watching me. I even turned my back on him.*

The thought made her shiver.

"Did—you—hear—that?" Billy stammered, choking on the air.

Jessica stopped thinking and opened her ears. All she was hearing was the wind blowing outside and things shaking in the yard. "I don't hear anything."

Brian was seated next to her, his legs out in front of him, sort of hunched with a blank expression. "It's not the driver."

Jessica looked at him. "What?"

"I said: it's not the driver. I thought it was the driver because that clown out there is wearing the same outfit, but that's not the same *face*. No, that's not the driver, the driver was nice. That thing out there … I don't know what that is."

Jessica placed a hand on his shoulder and he jumped.

"Sorry," she said.

"Travis," Brian said blankly. "He's dead—he's really *dead*."

Billy started crying again. "I want my mom. I want my mom."

Jessica told him to quiet down but felt bad about saying it. She wanted her mother too, and her father. She wanted to click her heels and slip away in a cloud of smoke. She wanted to be anywhere but this house which was dark and the phones weren't working. Most of all, she wished she had never come over here. She wished she would have gone with Jack instead. Over there, she would be in his arms, maybe not enjoying the night, but certainly not fearing she may not be here to enjoy the morning. No, she sat there, wishing she were never here.

"There it is again," Billy said, scooting further away from the door. "You hear it?"

The thing was, they all heard it. It was out there, something scratching along the walls just on the other side or down the hall, or maybe just below them. It sounded like a piece of metal furrowing the plaster. And each of them had an idea of what that metal was. In their heads, they were probably thinking of big knives or swords, blades forged over flames and hammered to precision on anvils; something medieval and spiked and narrow-edged. And wielding those bone-slicing implements was a clown; a skeletal imitation of a clown.

"I want it to stop," Billy said. "I can't take that noise anymore. It's outside that door. I can hear him, I can feel it out there. He wants me. I saw him looking at me before you grabbed, Jessica. He looked at me like I was something you eat. I know he was—Oh, God, I can't be here—I need my mommy—"

Jessica started trembling because that feeling of dread was worming through her bones like cancer, and it was starting to influence her limbs with shivers and spasms. She hated it. Hated being in this house. Hated Brian and Billy because they were too young and needed someone to watch over them. She wasn't a good person, she hated doing these gigs. She wasn't prepared for taking care of kids, she can barely hold the strings of her life above the waves. She needed to get the hell out of this. And right then, that window was looking good.

"Listen, do you hear it—you can hear him right?" Billy said.

Jessica snapped out of her mind.

Brian sat forward.

"What the hell is that?" she asked in a low voice that might have been mistaken for a thought.

They were waiting in silence, waiting for that noise to come back and verify to them that they indeed were hearing it. And when it came back, it was more than they could handle.

CHAPTER 14

One minute the wall was a solid sheet of white paint with pictures on it, the next, it was rupturing up the middle like an earthquake was cracking it. And, to say that it was an earthquake was pretty similar to how it would sound if it were. They all heard it before the wall started separating like a pair of giant claws were breaching it and pulling it apart. It was a motor, a noxious sounding, gas-operated motor. It was a familiar noise, and growing up in Oak Falls, you got used to that sound come winter when the cold was settling over the town, and the need for firewood arose. Yeah, it was a chainsaw, and its teeth were chewing a ragged line up that wall as if it were made of clay. Smoke billowed from the paint as the drywall cracked apart and broke out in big chunks. The room was soon a white cloud that smelled like gasoline and oil.

Jessica was screaming, her hands pressed to her head, her body shaking watching that big chain-edged arm work up the wall in a slowly meandering seam.

Brian was crying and searching his parent's

drawers, shouting that his father had a pistol somewhere in there, but he didn't know where it was.

Billy was hysterical and screaming and bouncing over the room, crying about how the clown was coming to eat him and do other things to him, he knew it was, he felt it. His voice was cracking in strident wails, and his feet were leaving the ground as he pouted and jumped and screamed and stammered.

"Somebody help me!" Billy cried. He raced over to Jessica, curled up against her. "Help me Jessica, please help me!"

His arms were locked around her waist and she tried pushing him away from her. But that look he gave her made her heart weak. She *loved* this kid, *loved* Brian—and Travis too. These were her brothers; that's what she felt. And she couldn't let anything bad happen to them.

The wall was coming apart and the saw had almost reached the ceiling. But, before it did, the clown stepped through the breach, and everyone screamed, and the smell of voided bowels was in the air; it fused with the fumes of gasoline and smoke and fresh sundered timber.

Brian plastered himself to the back wall, forcing his body against it so hard he was hoping he would fall through to the outside.

Billy was clutching Jessica and his crying went above her own peals.

The chainsaw charged and cycled and the clown

menaced the three with it; jabbing the end towards them and laughing. Yes, Bones the Clown was laughing about it all because it was amusing to him. It was that hollow, reverberating laughter of the damned, as if a hundred souls were in his throat, mocking these others; it was a demon chorus, shattering the room with its wicked dissonance.

Jessica's heart was racing, her breathing had paused. She didn't want to die. She couldn't die. She was still young and had dreams of moving out of Oak Falls and one day *being* somebody in another city, another state. Maybe someplace warmer with a beach. And she couldn't have all that if she was dead. So, she made a decision. She leaned down and bit Billy's arm until she drew blood. He screamed and let go of her. She shoved at him and he staggered in surprise towards the clown, screaming. The saw caught his fall, and each tooth on that chain cycled through his chest until that long guide bar sank into his body. And when that happened, he was lifted off the ground, held in the air as the chain rotated and clogged the teeth with meat and bone; the room was showered in gore and raining blood. The whites of the walls, of the bedsheets, of Jessica and Brian's faces, were oiled a greasy red. The clown was still laughing and Billy was nearly severed to the crotch. Both halves were flapping like rose petals and spraying blood and fluids. It was a bloodbath. A lake of red was rising off the carpet as blood continued to shower and add volume to it.

Jessica made her move and raced out of the hole

in the wall.

Brian ran after her, a bloody, stumbling, crying figure.

They were both down the hall, near the stairs, when the chainsaw went silent.

Instinctively they turned, thinking they would see the clown standing there, but all that was there was that black hole in the wall and the sound of water dripping somewhere. But it wasn't water, and they knew that.

Brian took hold of her arms and started shaking her. "*You killed him, you killed my friend! You're a bitch, I hate you—I fucking hate you!*"

But she wasn't listening. Her eyes were on the hole in the wall. Behind her sockets flashed the image of Billy rising off the ground and his body blowing open and spilling everything inside of it on the ground and ceiling and window and walls and bed. It was everywhere. She saw Travis too, a splayed-out, empty-headed thing on the table.

Her ruminations were a flashing reel behind her eyes, and in those ruinous, crimson-laden glimpses, she never saw the clown approach her, or heard the screams of Brian at the bottom of the stairs, telling her to run—to hurry and run down the stairs.

She came back after her eyes—and her mind— flooded her with awareness. In her pupils was that man. A haunted, scarecrow clown of bone white. The grin was a malicious gash on his face, and so exhausted with the terror, she was unable to summon a scream as those teeth clamped around her throat and tore out a hole as big as a fist. Her hands flew up to her neck, blocking the blood that was expelled in a rapid wave down her body, but it was no use, and already her body was weakening at an accelerated rate. So unaware of the pain as the numbness settled into her, she never felt those shark's teeth scraping the meat off her face, and gashing her crown and neck. And she was dead by the time Bones the Clown picked her up and held her body over his head and tossed her down below where her bones cracked against the tiles.

CHAPTER 15

Brian collapsed to his knees. The sound of her bones shattering was a hideous sound, and his legs went to sauce because of it. The way she landed, on her back, her arms out to her side, her head —what there was left of it—twisted unnaturally, facing him, was staring right into him. And he was looking back into that blooded, meatless mask; to the blood-clotted sockets where her beautiful green eyes used to sparkle. Brian was sobbing in heaving gasps, his face a gloss of tears. It hurt to breathe, but he couldn't sit there and wallow over what had happened to Jessica and his friends, because that clown was lurking down those steps in the most awful animation. The clown's face was bloody and wet and ropes of drool were threaded to its chin. It was grinning at him like it could taste him, and Brian started heaving as the air in his lungs emptied.

It was like watching a horror movie, and that's what this was; it had to be. He was dreaming. Yes, that's what happened. He fell asleep. Right now he was curled up on that warm couch with Jessica next to him, both of them asleep. Billy and Travis were upstairs, playing commando or Castlevania, leaving them in peace. Because the idea that he was sitting in a dark foyer on his knees, watching this slinking, skulking, bone pale clown with a bloody face leering at him, was too much for his young mind to validate. It was a nightmare; and maybe, just maybe that is what this was. A nightmare, something playing in his mind as he sat there folded up on the couch.

But he knew it wasn't.

It was real, real as that clown now standing over him, blood from his chin spotting Brian on the face. Brian fell back onto the tiles, and Bones the Clown brought something out of the silky, black and white jumper. It was a knife, but not a normal blade, it was a fillet knife, Brian recognized it. It was his father's. Another tool he must have gotten from the shed. It was a long, narrow-bladed knife too, finely honed to skin.

Bones slashed the air above Brian's face and Brian screeched. Bones started laughing in that loathsome, beastly cacophony as he continued to fan the air above the boy's screams.

Brian placed his hands over his face, afraid of what would happen if that edge hit him. Balled up as he was, he was shivering and crying and screaming for his parents so bad he was unaware that the clown had stopped laughing.

After a moment, Brian peeked between his fingers, and after not seeing that clown above him, he moved his hands away from his face.

Bones was gone, but not for good, because he was

over there, standing over Jessica, over her corpse, and the silky clown jumper was broken open down the middle. Jessica's clothes were a tatter of ribbons ringing her body. Brian could see her breasts and her thigh down to her legs. Bones was between her ankles, and he was pulling on himself.

Brian wanted to run, but so absorbed in the terror of what he was watching, what he had survived, he felt anchored; a broken heap. His eyes had darkened and his mind was reeling, alive with horrors.

Bones stared right into his eyes with those black sockets, and Brian was shaking. The clown was bloody and terrible and what he was doing to himself; the intent of it all, was atrocious. Brian knew what that clown was fixing to do. It was going to rape Jessica. But, no, it wasn't rape, it went beyond that now. It was a necrotic violation. She was cold and clogged and dead, and Bones was looking down on her like she was fresh and alive, or maybe just the right flavor. He lowered himself over her like an animal; because that's what he was. An animal, some regression from man to primate to beast. Beyond that, he was a monster, a ghoul, a violator. A desecrater. His face traced her body and his nostrils flared above her sex. His tongue was long and sinuous and trailed her curves and dips and slid between her thighs. The sound was awful. Coming up, his tongue wet, his hand below, working himself, he licked up her belly to between her breasts and, striking like a rattler, his teeth clamped her nipple and sheared it, taking it into his mouth where he chewed and swallowed.

Brian screamed, and it was that scream that compelled his release from the binding hypnotism of dread and horror. Rising, he raced to the door, threw back the locks, and was outside, in the windy, black night.

CHAPTER 16

Brian's flight was a shrieking madness in the wind. Outside his home the night was a solid mass and angles were distorted by a mind where sanity was usurped and replaced; reformed with illusions and voids brooding with frightful shapes and doors leading to dreadful planes; places where children screamed and were fed into the masticating chamber of steel teeth. Brian was no longer in Oak Falls, but in a terrible, inverted dimension where familiarity was alien and all around him was a blackness occulted by hideous sounds and moon-faced horrors, leaning figures, and demon winds.

The laughter was close, he could feel its heat pressing against him as if it were blowing from ovens. And he ran alongside the wall of his home, because outside, out front, beyond his home, was a territory that fell away into an ogreish abyss, and the hills were no mercy for his flight because their grids were transposed with illimitable leagues of hideous, brain shattering nightmares.

Racing along the fence of his yard, he heard the

patter of naked feet on grass, and he turned briefly, and filled in his widened eyes was the shambling Clown. But, it was worse somehow. A transmutation stretched his height and his shadow leaned against the wall of the home, a great, looming amorphous blot of ink that writhed and reshaped as a balloon animal is shaped. And Brian screamed as the shadow seemed to leer over him and beckon him with fingers that were not fingers but the crooked talons of some midnight horror from the screen. The shadow was sentient, and Brian feared it would detach and reach down for him and drag him screaming into a world of shifting shadows; to be absorbed in the folds of black waves.

Running, crying, screaming, his foot caught the humped root of a maple outside the fence of his yard. Reality swiftly returned to him in his descent to the ground. The world rushed back into focus and the wind, familiar as it was, blew into him and the Clown—yes, the Clown was there, only ten feet from where he sat and steadily nearing.

Bones the Clown's face was a twisted mask of blood and teeth that were clogged with meat. The silky clown jumper was open up in the middle and flapping with the wind. The knife was fused in his fist and its surface was no longer silver but matted with hair and smeared with blood and spotted in bits of yellow fat. His other hand was curled around the bloody shaft between his legs, and his fingers slid up the length and back, an oiled, pulsating rod. He neared the boy, and his excitement increased.

He was hungry, for Bones the Clown was never satiated, and he could smell the boy's blood and that smell enhanced his grin into an impossible width of dripping red fangs.

Raw as his throat was, Brian tried to scream, but what came out was a choking sob. It sounded wizened and old, like lungs walled with disease.

The Clown came closer, and his hand never stopped and the blade point lowered over the boy's head. A foot away now, the Clown stood. An appalling totem of pale effulgence.

All of the horrors of the night flooded into Brian's memory. A quick flash showed him the empty skull of Travis, the mutilated destruction of Billy, and the chainsaw; Jessica violated and consumed in the foyer. In a brief rupture from the night and its terror, Brian felt the enraging power of survival. He lashed out with a tight fist and cracked Bones the Clown beneath the throbbing crown of his member.

Bones stood unmoved, his face impassive, but in his eyes shone a hint of pain. It was a fleeting spark, but it was just enough for Brian to make his escape.

On his feet, he pushed past the immobile Clown and ran back towards the front of his house, mindless of where he ran. All he could think of was the safety of his home, a place that was no longer safe, but the feel of walls and security is what he sought, and out here, under the black sky and blowing winds, was vulnerable. Brian needed to be inside, back inside where he could hide in that spot he used to hide when his parents would fight and they would never find him. Yes, he needed to go there and avoid the wrath of the boogeyman. Because that Clown, that skull-faced haunter, was angered by him, and would soon come after him and feed on his corpse, then slake his necrophiliac urges.

As Brian rounded the corner of his home, two shapes on the front lawn filled his eyes. Tall black shapes that were shouting at him. Blue and red light flashed off the face of homes and the sight was disorienting to the mind.

"Son, are you okay?" one of the tall shapes inquired. "You have blood on you—are you hurt? What happened here?" the voice was strong, authoritative.

Brian shuddered, overcome with the safety these two men represented. They were police officers, and their presence was the sword he much required to fend off this accursed Clown. His body shook and broke down into tears, but he managed to raise an arm and point a finger behind him. "A clown—" he stuttered "—a clown is after me. It killed everybody."

One of the men came forward, lowering his gun, and he reached out to the boy. "Give me your hand, son."

Brian took the man's hand and was now being walked back to the police car. The door was thrown open and Brian was settled inside.

"I'm going to check on the house, you'll be safe here."

Brian only stared at the man, mute.

The door shut behind the man as he trailed back

up the house to be with his partner.

—

"Terry, take it slow in there," Officer Stevens said.

Terry was in first and after just two steps, his flashlight fell on a pile of something that caused him to reel and stagger back out into the night.

"Jesus …"

Stevens looked at him. "What—what is it?"

Terry shook his head. "It's awful.

Stevens stepped inside, his light showing him a pool of gore. A woman was laying there, her head twisted off. She was mostly a stick figure of red bones, her entrails scattered around her.

Stevens backed up, back outside.

"God, what the hell happened here?"

Stevens shrugged, then looked over to the patrol car. The boy's face was pressed to the glass, his expression a white mask and nothing more. But, he was pointing at something.

"Terry, on me."

They moved around the house, their flashlights burning holes in the dark. The wind was still blowing, but it was coming in gusts. Stevens was in the lead, his shoulder an inch from the fence. His light fell on something back where the fence cornered at the end, and he raised his pistol.

"Freeze!" he shouted. "Oak Falls Police Department!"

Terry came around his partner, adding his own light to the object. It looked like an elbow and part of a clown outfit.

"Come on out—now!" Stevens shouted.

They waited a second before Terry pointed with his gun like he was thinking about heading on over there and taking this person by force.

Stevens nodded, indicating he would cover his advance. The two moved in unity, and when Terry got ten feet to the elbow, the arm swung out with a long curving red blade, and the clown-covered body came with it.

Terry screamed at the image of the bloody face and his gun jumped in his fist and shells glittered from the slide. Stevens, too, emptied each chamber of his revolver until the cylinder was smoking.

They looked at each other, then put their lights on the clown. There were big red holes on his back from the bullet impacts.

"Terry, turn him over."

Terry shoved at the clown with the tip of his boot.

"Holy Jesus," Stevens said.

"What? Who is he?"

Stevens shook his head. "Tony, from Crazy Clown Pizza."

"You sure?"

"I've arrested the man enough to know his face well." Still, Stevens looked stumped on the issue. "But, why? This makes no sense. I mean he's a thief an all, but ... doing something like that to the poor girl in the house ... don't add up."

"I guess some people just break, sir."

"Get on the radio, get—wait, what the hell was

that?"

Terry heard it too.

Both men ran back to the front of the house. They stared at the gaping hole in the back window of the police cruiser. There were stripes of blood down the white painted door. A trail of glass leading off … towards the creek.

The men started to follow the glass chips when they both froze at the sound ringing out of the woods. It was a hellish, high-pealing scream of agony. But it was choked and throttled sounding, like somebody losing their voice.

"The boy!" Stevens shouted.

Already they were running for those woods, determined to reach that boy and render him the help he needed. Because he needed it badly. The way he was screaming and shrieking in those black woods, it was like something was tearing him apart. Maybe an animal, maybe something worse. But whatever it was, it had him in there and it was doing awful things to him. Stevens and Terry were almost hesitant to enter, the sound was appalling and damn atrocious to ears that were not accustomed to such grisly sounds.

But in there they went. Their flashlights tunneled the dark and their guns, freshly loaded, were raised just below their timid glares. They half-expected something to jump out from behind the trees, but that was ludicrous, but maybe not.

The screaming stopped before it started again with a bone-trembling shiver. Stevens picked up his pace and headed over to where he thought the boy could be. They had just crossed the creek and pushed up an incline, and when it flattened out, that's when Stevens saw it. Sitting right there in the blade of his flashlight. He saw the boy, or what was left of him. He was mostly just a ragged, chewed-up thing, his face gone—scooped out and hollow. His pants were gone and his legs were open in some obscene way. Most of his belly was ripped out and missing—just missing. There was a trail of something red and it wound out further than their lights reached.

"I ain't following that," Terry whispered, his eyes wide, his gun shaking.

Stevens didn't say it, but he wasn't either, because he was already backing up slowly, getting ready to run out of there. He turned to do just that when something laughed, and it wasn't a normal mirthful cackle, but something unnatural and wrathful and hideous and evil. Yes, evil, because that's what it was. It was the corrupting laughter of a demon. It carried with the wind, and its resonance coiled the oaks and reflected hauntingly off the giant boles. It seemed to rise into the night and divert the wind.

Stevens and Terry ran, ran out of there screaming and shouting, until they were back by their car, panting and listening, yes listening because the laughter never stopped.

AFTERWORD

Thank you for reading and purchasing! I hope you enjoyed the book. This was a spur-of-the-moment piece. I wrote this in three days. The word count is a pinch over 22k. I'm very happy with it. I wanted to write this with a bit of an extreme angle to it. But I also didn't want to lose that grindhouse, 80ish feel either. The child in this story was named after me, which was done on purpose because I released this as a special story for my birthday. Drew Stepek, from GODLESS, asked if I wanted to secure the 7th of September to release something. I told him I didn't have anything, but I could throw something together, and thats how this gruesome piece was generated. It was heavily influenced by Puppet Combo's Babysitter Bloodbath, also, movies like Clownhouse (1989) and Terrifer (2016). I plan to release the fifth installment of the Slasherback Series in November. It will be a sequel to Thanksgiving Day Massacre (II). I will also be releasing a couple of other projects before then too. Thank you to all who support me. Your kind words and friendships are the inspiration that encourages my pen. Again, thank you.

Printed in Great Britain
by Amazon